Arthur W. Pinero

The Hobby-horse

A Comedy, in Three Acts

Arthur W. Pinero

The Hobby-horse
A Comedy, in Three Acts

ISBN/EAN: 9783744769105

Printed in Europe, USA, Canada, Australia, Japan

Cover: Foto ©Andreas Hilbeck / pixelio.de

More available books at **www.hansebooks.com**

THE HOBBY-HORSE

A COMEDY

In Three Acts

By ARTHUR W. PINERO

LONDON: WILLIAM HEINEMANN

MDCCCXCII

INTRODUCTORY NOTE

SIX years ago dramatic conventionality exercised an
even greater tyranny than it does to-day, and British
playgoers were less prepared than now to look favourably
upon any effort to resist it. That the persons in a play
should be dealt with according to the probabilities of
actual life, when these clashed with the dictates of
theatrical custom and "poetical justice," was not to be
endured. The expectations of an audience were held
sacred, and were not to be tampered with. They were
as inexorable as the laws of the Medes and Persians, and
any dramatist who had the temerity to bring down his
curtain without having first made all his sympathetic
characters happy might expect little favour. But even
at that time Mr. Pinero was always inclined to fly in the
face of the theatrically conventional in some way or
another, and he actually dared to write a play in which
a young clergyman, for whom the deep sympathy of the
audience was enlisted, was permitted to fall innocently
and honourably in love with a married woman whom he
had thought to be single, and to suffer pain on her
account, without the husband being conveniently killed
off in the last act to prepare the way for the clergyman's
expected matrimonial happiness. And this play Mr.

Pinero, having his own dramatic purpose in view, described as a comedy.

"The Hobby-Horse" was produced at the St. James's Theatre, under the management of Mr. Hare and Mr. Kendal, on October 23, 1886, and it was acted until February 26, 1887, one hundred and nine performances being given in all. The following is a copy of the programme of the first representation :—

ST. JAMES'S THEATRE.

LESSEES AND MANAGERS, MR. HARE AND MR. KENDAL.

THIS EVENING, SATURDAY, OCTOBER 23rd, 1886,

At 8 o'clock,

WILL BE ACTED

AN ORIGINAL COMEDY IN THREE ACTS, CALLED

THE HOBBY-HORSE,

WRITTEN BY

A. W. PINERO.

REV. NOEL BRICE	Mr. HERBERT WARING.
MR. SPENCER JERMYN . . .	Mr. HARE.
MR. PINCHING	Mr. C W. SOMERSET.
MR. SHATTOCK	Mr. MACKINTOSH.
MR. PEWS	Mr. HENDRIE.
MR. LYMAN	Mr. W. M. CATHCART.
MR. MOULTER	Mr. THOMAS.
TOM CLARK	Mr. FULLER MELLISH.
HEWETT	Mr. ALBERT SIMS.
TINY LANDON	Master REED.

MRS. SPENCER JERMYN . . . . Mrs. KENDAL.
MRS. PORCHER . . . . . Mrs. GASTON MURRAY.
MISS MOXON . . . . . Mrs. B. TREE.
BERTHA . . . . . . Miss WEBSTER.
MRS. LANDON . . . . . Miss B. HUNTLEY.

ACT I.

A CHAPTER OF PHILANTHROPY.

At Mr. JERMYN'S.

Garden of Odlum House, Over-Lessingham, near Newmarket.

ACT II.

A CHAPTER OF SENTIMENT.

Mr. BRICE'S *Lodgings:*

Overlooking the Church of St. Jacob's-in-the-East.

ACT III.

A CHAPTER OF EXPIATION.

Odlum House again; the Morning Room.

THE SCENERY PAINTED BY THE ARTIST TO THE THEATRE,
MR. HARFORD.

Though it would be unjust to write this play down a
failure it was not exactly a success. That large section
of the playgoing public which expects only to laugh at a
comedy, was puzzled between the comic and the sentimental aspects of the story, and therefore the attendance
at the theatre gradually diminished. On the other hand,
there were many who saw that this play was intended as
a satire on those false philanthropic fads which are
a sign of a sentimental age; who recognised in the

abortive love affair of the young curate, not an injustice done to their theatrical sympathies, not a capricious piece of cruelty on the part of the author, but the dramatic means by which the disastrous consequences of misdirected philanthropy were to be emphasised. That the play should have been called a comedy provoked the ire of some of the critics, who promptly repeated the charge of cynicism which has so often been hurled against Mr. Pinero for his efforts to be as true to life as the restricted conditions of dramatic composition destined for the stage will allow. And to-day, if you ask Mr. Pinero to define a comedy, he will playfully tell you it is a farce written by a deceased author.

Perhaps "The Hobby-Horse," in its defiance of the conventional demand for wholesale conjugal happiness in the last act, though an ample supply was conceded, was a little before its time ; perhaps in 1886 it still required the Ibsen controversy to clear the theatrical air for the acceptance of such a progressive step as the sacrifice of the curate's feelings and future domestic comfort to the artistic design and satirical purpose of the play. Had "The Hobby-Horse" been produced at the present time, who knows but it might possibly have met with greater success, for though we may still quarrel about the definition of comedy, we do not still insist on every occasion that everybody shall be made absolutely and irrevocably happy before curtain-fall.

MALCOLM C. SALAMAN.

THE PERSONS OF THE PLAY

MR. SPENCER JERMYN

MRS. SPENCER JERMYN

MR. PINCHING

MISS MOXON

REV. NOEL BRICE

BERTHA

TOM CLARK

MRS. PORCHER

SHATTOCK

PEWS

LYMAN

MOULTER

MRS. LANDON

TINY LANDON

HEWITT

THE FIRST ACT

A CHAPTER OF PHILANTHROPY

THE SECOND ACT

A CHAPTER OF SENTIMENT

THE THIRD ACT

A CHAPTER OF EXPIATION

THE HOBBY-HORSE

THE FIRST ACT.

A CHAPTER OF PHILANTROPHY.

The scene is the garden and exterior of a picturesque old country-house, with gables and porch all overgrown with flowers, the residence of MR. SPENCER JERMYN. *It is a bright May morning.*

SHATTOCK *comes cautiously along the garden walk, followed by* PEWS. SHATTOCK *is a bony, ungainly-looking man of about forty, with high shoulders, rounded back, close-cropped head set forward, and a sallow, keen-eyed face;* PEWS *is a snub-nosed, red-faced, fat little man. Both are dressed horseyly, and have a very broken-down appearance.*

SHATTOCK.

[*Turning sharply upon* PEWS.] Sssh! Can't you turn off that music?

PEWS.

[*Panting and wiping his forehead.*] No, I cannot—if you allood to my breathing a bit heavy.

A

SHATTOCK.

You're a nice broken-winded gentleman to bring out on a quiet delicate expedition. Didn't I tell you, Edward Pews, that it ain't our book to meet the ladies? Breathe in your 'at, man; breathe in your 'at.

PEWS.

You knew I was a roarer when you brought me here, Samuel. I 'ave been so ever since I got ducked at Doncaster in '84.

SHATTOCK.

[*Crouching on the steps and looking into the house.*] There they are—I see 'em, all of 'em—'aving their morning feed. Mr. Spencer Jermyn is a glaucin' at the newspaper—a little curious about the prices for the Grand Pree apparently. Mrs. Jermyn is a toying with a hegg. Oh, you beauty! Who's the other? Oh, Miss Moxon, the lady stayin' in the 'ouse, makes a bad third. All right—Jermyn'll show directly. He said he'd be 'appy to see myself and friend this morning at 10 A.M.

PEWS.

Did he! Then why the dooce are we sneakin' up to his 'ouse, huggin' the rails instead of takin' the middle o' the course fair and open?

SHATTOCK.

I'll tell you, Edward—then p'rhaps you'll breathe a little peacefuller. You've seen this 'ere Spencer Jermyn?

PEWS.

At pretty nigh hevery race-meeting for the last ten years. I've see him at Lincoln—I've see him at Liverpool—I've see him at the Epsom Spring—I've see him 'ere at Newmarket—I've see him at the Epsom Summer—I've see him——

SHATTOCK.

Very well, you've *see* him—that's enough. D'ye know the party in question?

PEWS.

I can't say as we've ever chummed, but I've heered him classed as a generous patron of the turf and a good and game thoroughbred Henglish gent.

SHATTOCK.

You've hit it—you've enoomerated Spencer Jermyn's points more than accurate. He's a man wot loves the 'orse and all them wot has to do with the 'orse—he loves racin' and sport and pluck, and he's got a open 'and for any broken-down sportsman. Some say that hintellectnally Mr. Spencer Jermyn wouldn't pass the Vet. Well, *I* ain't going to howl about that. If Spencer Jermyn takes a lovin' fancy to Samuel Shattock, ex-jockey, ex-trainer, ex-bookmaker, hex—hex——

PEWS.

Hex-welsher.

SHATTOCK.

That's a friendly comment, Edward! [*Looking into the house.*] Hullo, they're stirrin'.

PEWS.

But you 'aven't told me, Sam, why you want to fight shy of the women folk.

SHATTOCK.

Why! Because Mr. Spencer Jermyn has gone and married a lady who don't know a 'orse from a 'am sandwich; a female with no more lovin' sympathy for the Turf and them wot lives by it than—than the chaplain of York Prison.

PEWS.

Hush! drop a wail over the past, Sam.

SHATTOCK.

"Always keep out of the way of the ladies, Mr. Shattock," says Jermyn to me. "Mrs. Jermyn has no eyes for anything but her little ragged urchins."

PEWS.

What's he mean by *that?*

SHATTOCK.

Why, he's married a woman with a craze. She's a—a—a—a philant'ropist.

PEWS.

Crikey!

SHATTOCK.

Never 'appy but wot she's picking up dirty little boys and girls and takin' them home and washing and combing 'em, and giving 'em cake and sermon. As if *his* philant'ropy wasn't as good as *her* philan-

t'ropy ! As if *we* didn't want washin' and combin'
as much—ay, more than the dirtiest boys and girls
in England ! Look out ! [Mrs. Landon, *a poor
widow, comes up the walk, leading* Tiny Landon, *a
small boy.*] There ! What did I tell you ! Here's
one of Mrs. Jermyn's little devils, ready to take the
bread out of an honest man's mouth.

[Shattock *steps forward to meet* Mrs. Landon.]

MRS. LANDON.

I beg your pardon, sir—I want for to see the lady,
Mrs. Jermyn.

SHATTOCK.

Tall, fair lady ? Went down that theer avenue
about twenty minutes ago. Am I correct in what I
am sayin', Mr. Pews ?

PEWS.

I certainly *see* a tall, fair lady goin' down the avenue, a carrying a red plush bag with a monygram
on it.

MRS. LANDON.

Eh, but she told me not to fail to bring my little
boy this morning. I am that disappointed.

SHATTOCK.

She was similarly anxious for to see Mr. Pews—I
'ave brought 'im miles and miles. We're all in the
same basket, seems to me.

[Hewett, *a groom, comes from the house.*]

HEWETT.

[*To* Pews *and* Shattock.] Hullo, what do you
want?

SHATTOCK.

We're a' waitin' for to see Mr. Jermyn, Mr. Hewett. Don't hasten him, sir—our time's our own.

HEWETT.

Oh, good-morning, Mrs. Landon. Mistress said I was to take you and Tiny to her room d'rectly you came.

MRS. LANDON.

These gentlemen thought they saw her go out— they must have been mistaken.

HEWETT.

'Taint the first time in their lives they've been mistaken, I dare say. Come along o' me.

[MRS. LANDON *follows* HEWETT *up the steps to the house.*]

SHATTOCK.

[*Cuffing* TINY, *who runs after his mother.*] You get shown in, do you—you pushing little cad!

[MR. JERMYN, *a smart, dapper little man of forty-five or fifty, with a sporting appearance, comes through the porch and meets* HEWETT, MRS. LANDON, *and* TINY *on the steps.*]

SPENCER JERMYN.

Ah, Mrs. Landon, how do you do? Getting over your trouble?

MRS. LANDON.

Slowly, sir.

SPENCER JERMYN.

Your boy doesn't grow much—put him into a
stable and make a jockey of him. [MRS. LANDON
and TINY *go inside with* HEWETT.] Lord bless me!
Another rackety little imp running about the place
—we're swarming with 'em. Ah, if my scheme
should by any chance satisfy Diana's philanthropic
cravings, what a relief it would be!

SHATTOCK.

[*Meeting* JERMYN *as he descends the steps.*] Good-
mornin', Mr. Spencer Jermyn, sir.

SPENCER JERMYN.

Ah, Mr. Shattock, you're punctual, I'm glad to see.

SHATTOCK.

Yes, Mr. Jermyn, sir, and I've ventured for to
bring with me the other deservin' case I mentioned.
Mr. Hedward Pews, formerly a boy in John Gor-
ton's stable—he rode Hysteria for Lord Oscott in
the Hoaks so fur back as '56—being suspended
from riding at Goodwood in '61 on a unjust charge
of 'orrid language at the post, he took to drink and
put on flesh rapid. In proof whereof I ask you to
look at 'im. Since that time he has been various,
but never lucky. He——

SPENCER JERMYN.

All right—all right. What has he been doing
lately?

PEWS.

Selling tips in envelopes, sir—and doin' poorly, my voice not tellin' after the fust hour.

SPENCER JERMYN.

Can he refer me to anybody?

SHATTOCK.

Can he refer you to anybody!

PEWS.

Can I refer you to anybody! Ho!

SHATTOCK.

[*Admiringly.*] Can you refer him to anybody! [*They look uneasily at each other.*] Can he refer you to—h'm!—well, in a sort of way, Mr. Pews gives *me* as a refryence.

SPENCER JERMYN.

Oh—well, I'll make inquiries. All I can say for the present is, I don't dislike your friend's face. [PEWS *wipes his face carefully with a dirty handkerchief.*] And now I had better explain, Mr. Shattock, why I desired to see you this morning. Sit down—don't mind me—sit down. [SHATTOCK *and* PEWS *sit side by side on a garden bench.*] I will walk about. I am so excitedly interested in my scheme that I really cannot discuss it sitting down.

SHATTOCK.

We will hear you out, sir—we will hear you out.

PEWS.

You're a gentleman, sir—none better.

SPENCER JERMYN.

My scheme is this. Mrs. Jermyn, my wife, is a lady of a most charitable disposition. It is my fault entirely that I have comparatively little sympathy with the precise form of her generosity. However, that's nothing to do with you, my men.

SHATTOCK.

Go on, sir—we're 'earin' you.

SPENCER JERMYN.

Mrs. Jermyn, on the other hand, has no feeling for anything or anybody connected with the Turf or the Stable—no feeling except one of positive distaste.

PEWS.

Shame! Shame!

SPENCER JERMYN.

How dare you employ that ejaculation in reference to Mrs. Jermyn, sir? What do you mean by it, eh?

SHATTOCK.

[*To* PEWS.] Now I 'ope you're proud of yourself!

SPENCER JERMYN.

Mrs. Jermyn's prejudices are quite beyond not only the censure but the comprehension of such as ourselves.

SHATTOCK.

[*To* PEWS.] Because your face gets flattered you
go and lose your 'ead!

SPENCER JERMYN.

But I think, Mr. Shattock, that I have discovered
a method of blending Mrs. Jermyn's notions of
philanthropy with a pet plan of my own to benefit
some of the waifs and strays connected with the
noble pastime which is more than my hobby, which
is my existence.

SHATTOCK.

Well spoken!

SPENCER JERMYN.

There is a farm-house of mine which has been
vacant for a long time, about five miles from here,
at Shodly Heath—a very commodious, well built
dwelling. Perhaps you know it?

SHATTOCK.

A 'ouse painted yaller cream colour?

SPENCER JERMYN.

That's it. [*Seeing* JERMYN *take out a cigar*, SHAT-
TOCK *and* PEWS *simultaneously produce their clay
pipes.*] Now my notion is to fit and furnish this
house substantially and usefully, and to endow it as
a Home for about twenty decayed jockeys and
stablemen, men like yourselves, who have outlived
their chances on the turf and fallen on bad days.
There, Mr. Shattock, what do you think of that?

SHATTOCK.

Tell me, mister—are you hentering us for the temperance stakes?

SPENCER JERMYN.

How dare you put a question like that? Where's your gratitude for the bare idea?

SHATTOCK.

I was a thinkin' of Mr. Pews—too little is as bad as too much for a man like Edward Pews.

SPENCER JERMYN.

We'll discuss that by and by. The point is, Mr. Shattock, can you find twenty men who would be willing to lead honest, sober, decent lives?

SHATTOCK.

Well, off hand I shouldn't like for to pledge myself to sich a undertaking.

SPENCER JERMYN.

Men with some good sterling qualities in them behind all their faults and weaknesses.

SHATTOCK.

Well, you see I dessay I've rather spoilt you by showing you me and Mr. Pews fust. However, you leave this 'ere to me—and if there is on the face of this yer earth twenty honest broken-down sportsmen willing for to be kep' free and liberal I'll bring 'em to the post fit and fine.

SPENCER JERMYN.

Thank you—thank you. It's a grand scheme! I long to break it to Mrs. Jermyn—if she takes to it why, ha, ha! who knows, we may see her at Ascot yet!

[PINCHING, *a pleasant but rather weak-looking young man, in riding costume comes up the walk.*]

PINCHING.

How are you, Jermyn?

SPENCER JERMYN.

My dear Pinching.

PINCHING.

I'm behind my time—the mare lost a shoe, so I had to leave her at Lessingham and walk on. Are these gentlemen two of your *protégés?*

SPENCER JERMYN.

[*With pride.*] Yes. You're smiling, Pinching—don't, my boy, don't! I can't get you to treat this matter with professional earnestness. Er—um—Mr. Shattock, this is Mr. Ralph Pinching, of Newmarket—my solicitor.

[*The men bow uncomfortably.*]

PEWS.

Oh, crikey!

SHATTOCK.

[*Under his breath.*] 'Ere's a element to creep in.

SPENCER JERMYN.

Now, my men, I am leaving here this morning, almost immediately, and it is possible that I shall be away for nearly a month. But during my absence, Mr. Shattock, you will communicate with Mr. Pinching as if he were myself—he has my full instructions. [HEWETT *comes from the house.*] Hewett, don't forget I go to town by the twelve-fifteen. Put Romper in the cart.

HEWETT.

Yes, sir.

SPENCER JERMYN.

And give these men something to eat and drink.

SHATTOCK.

[*To* HEWETT.] Now you've got to show *us* in.

HEWETT.

Yes—*kitchen.*

SHATTOCK.

Cad!

[HEWETT *goes towards the house with* SHATTOCK *and* PEWS.]

PINCHING.

And now, my dear Jermyn, I've something really serious to talk to you about.

SPENCER JERMYN.

Good gracious, Pinching ; serious !

PINCHING.

Yes—you shall find me your man of business in real earnest for a few moments.

SPENCER JERMYN.

Lord bless me, Pinching, you don't mean——

PINCHING.

That I have some news of your boy, Allan? Yes, I think so.

SPENCER JERMYN.

My boy! my boy! Get on, sir! get on! For heaven's sake, don't go to sleep about it. It isn't that I'm in a hurry to hear anything of that scamp of a boy, but I have to catch the twelve-fifteen—God bless him!   [PINCHING *produces a pocket-book.*]

PINCHING.

Now tell me, Jermyn—when did you quarrel and part with your son? I particularly want dates.

SPENCER JERMYN.

Certainly—it was just before the Middle Park Plate——

PINCHING.

No, no, please—legally, that is not a perfect date.

SPENCER JERMYN.

Well, it was about six months before my marriage to Diana.

PINCHING.

And you married the present Mrs. Jermyn a little over a year ago; come, that's better. [*Turning over some papers.*] Now, about the time this quarrel occurred, I find that a young man named Thomas Clark shipped himself on board the steamship Penguin, bound for the Australian ports, as a common sailor.

SPENCER JERMYN.

Pooh! On the wrong scent—that wouldn't be my boy Allan.

PINCHING.

This Thomas Clark left some clothes behind him at a lodging in the East of London.

SPENCER JERMYN.

Allan wouldn't have done that—on the wrong scent, sir.

PINCHING.

The landlady subsequently sought the advice of the Police as to her right to dispose of this property. It was ultimately sold, but there exists a memorandum on the Police books that some articles of apparel belonging to Mr. Thomas Clark were marked "A. J."

SPENCER JERMYN.

That's my boy!

PINCHING.

I fancied it might be.

SPENCER JERMYN.

Fancy! There's no fancy about it! You surely haven't let the matter drop? My dear Pinching, you are neglecting this business altogether—I could have managed it better myself. It's not professional!

PINCHING.

Pray be calm, Jermyn, and hear me out.

SPENCER JERMYN.

Excuse me, Pinching. I am much obliged to you for your energy in this affair. Go on.

PINCHING.

It appears that the boy signed articles with the owners to make four voyages in the Penguin.

SPENCER JERMYN.

And did he?

PINCHING.

Thomas Clark did—and finally discharged himself at the East India Docks about a month ago.

SPENCER JERMYN.

And where is he now?

PINCHING.

That is just what I am trying to find out.

SPENCER JERMYN.

Trying to find out! Rubbish, sir!

PINCHING.

What I *mean* to find out, if I can.

SPENCER JERMYN.

[*Taking* PINCHING'S *hand.*] Thank you, old fellow ; you are a good friend. Bring my boy back to me again, Pinching, for two reasons. .

PINCHING.

. Two reasons ?

SPENCER JERMYN.

Well, in the first place Diana has never seen him —and a woman ought to know what her son is like. And, secondly, Pinching, in our quarrel the boy was right and I was wrong.

PINCHING.

Dear me !

SPENCER JERMYN.

It was a serious business. He fancied Medusa for the Middle Park Plate and I had a strong liking for King Caraway. But he said that King Caraway wasn't fit to run without a respirator and that irritated me, Pinching, and we had hot words and I saw him go out at that gate, sir, and we never met again. And next day when I watched the racing I was still so indignant, Pinching, that I could hardly steady my glasses. But the boy was right, God bless him ! And I want to tell him what I felt when I saw that confounded King Caraway go to pieces at the Abingdon Dip, sir, while Medusa, my dear boy's fancy, romped in like a ballet-girl !

[MISS MOXON, *a prettily dressed young lady, appears in the porch.*]

B

MISS MOXON.

Mr. Pinching.

PINCHING.

Oh, how do you do, Miss Moxon?

MISS MOXON.

Mrs. Jermyn wants to know if you have break-
fasted.

PINCHING.

Yes—thank you.

MISS MOXON.

Oh, do come in! It is almost my last hour in
Odlum House, Mr. Pinching—I'm going away this
morning for good.

PINCHING.

Going away! No!

MISS MOXON.

[*To* JERMYN.] Will you give poor unfortunate me
a lift to the station to catch the twelve-fifteen, Mr.
Jermyn?

SPENCER JERMYN.

I'm sorry to assist at your departure, Miss Moxon.
However, I'll tell Hewett we'll go over in the carriage.

[JERMYN *leaves them, and, directly he is out of
sight,* MISS MOXON *runs down the steps and*
PINCHING *takes her hand.*]

PINCHING.

Going away, Miss Moxon!

Miss Moxon.

Yes; isn't it awful? And I am so happy here with Diana. I feel I shall never be happy again, Mr. Pinching—never, never, never.

Pinching.

But why are you going?

Miss Moxon.

[*Sitting.*] It is my duty.

Pinching.

[*Sitting close beside her.*] Duty!

Miss Moxon.

Duty.

[Jermyn *returns quickly.*]

Spencer Jermyn.

Oh, by the bye, Pinching—— [Pinching *and* Miss Moxon *rise guiltily. All three are embarrassed.*] I just wanted to say—er—um——[*Looking at* Miss Moxon.] Excuse me, Pinching—won't you?

Pinching.

Certainly, Jermyn.

Spencer Jermyn.

Don't tell Mrs. Jermyn this morning of our discoveries about my boy Allan.

Pinching.

Certainly not, if you don't wish it.

SPENCER JERMYN.

It is rather a sore subject between us; Diana always points to the loss of my boy as one of the evil results of horse-racing, and as I'm just going to divulge my scheme for the Jockeys' Home at Shodley Heath, I particularly want her to be in a good temper to-day. That's all, Pinching. [*Looking at* Miss Moxon.] Excuse my—my awkwardness, won't you? Charming woman, Miss Moxon. Er—h'm! I shan't see you again for five minutes, Pinching. [JERMYN *goes into the house.*]

Miss Moxon.

[*Strolling towards* PINCHING.] Were you saying anything to me, Mr. Pinching, when dear Mr. Jermyn came back?

PINCHING.

Oh, yes—why is it specially your duty to run away from friends who—who like you so well, Miss Moxon?

Miss Moxon.

Why, don't you know that I am a very, very poor woman, Mr. Pinching; that I had nothing-a-year settled on me by my parents, who died almost before I was born; and that I have been some sort of a governess ever since I could lisp, and shall remain one till I am qualified for an almshouse.

PINCHING.

No—I only know that you were a schoolfellow of Mrs. Jermyn's, and that you have been a guest at

Odlum House for the last three weeks, and that—
and that——

MISS MOXON.

Yes?

PINCHING.

And that my legal visits to Mr. Jermyn have lately
been very protracted.

MISS MOXON.

Thank you! You're the only lawyer I've ever
known—as well as this.

PINCHING.

You are the only governess I have ever known as
well as this.

MISS MOXON.

I never imagined a lawyer was so young.

PINCHING.

Oh, yes—it's only in books that we suffer from
chronic old age.

MISS MOXON.

After to-day, when I am far, far away from Odlum
House, I shall always think pleasantly of a lawyer.

PINCHING.

And I shall always think pleasantly of a governess.

MISS MOXON.

Of governesses in general, do you mean—or *a*
governess?

PINCHING.

A governess.

MISS MOXON.

[*Looking away.*] Then do you know any other governess?

PINCHING.

No!

MISS MOXON.

Oh!

[MRS. JERMYN, *a stately, handsome woman of about thirty, appears at the top of the steps leading* TINY LANDON *by the hand.*]

MRS. JERMYN.

Won't you come into the house, Mr. Pinching? Constance, dear, you said you would look after Mr. Pinching.

MISS MOXON.

I am doing so, Diana.
[MRS. JERMYN *and* TINY *come down the steps as* MISS MOXON *and* PINCHING *ascend.*]

PINCHING.

Thank you, Mrs. Jermyn. Am I too old to compete with this young gentleman for a permanent location at Odlum House?

MRS. JERMYN.

Ah, Mr. Pinching, don't *you* be unsympathetic. I fear my husband's indifference is contagious. Go in, please—I am looking for Mr. Jermyn. [MISS

Moxon *and* Pinching *go into the house.* Mrs. Jermyn *goes down upon her knees before the child, smoothing his hair and polishing his face with her handkerchief.*] There, my dear little fellow—the sight of you ought to soften any man's heart. Where *is* Spencer? Ah, Tiny—if you could but realise it— the success of a grand, a beautiful scheme depends upon the impression you make upon Mr. Jermyn.

Tiny Landon.

[*Trying to avoid the pocket-handkerchief.*] Oh, don't !
[Jermyn *enters and contemplates* Mrs. Jermyn *and th. child with annoyance.*]

Spencer Jermyn.

There's one of those beastly little boys. Diana, my darling, I'm afraid I shall have to say good-bye very soon.

Mrs. Jermyn.

And when am I to see you again, Spencer?

Spencer Jermyn.

H'm ! Well, Diana, as you know, I am going to Paris to-night for the Auteuil Steeplechase.

Mrs. Jermyn.

Oh !

Spencer Jermyn.

I shall remain over there till after the Grand Prix.

Mrs. Jermyn.

Ugh !

SPENCER JERMYN.

And then, my dear, I suppose I had better——

MRS. JERMYN.

Return home, Spencer?

SPENCER JERMYN.

Well, Diana, I was about to say that I had better then—er—um—push on to Ascot.

MRS. JERMYN.

And have you been as precise in your arrangements for *my* occupation, Spencer?

SPENCER JERMYN.

Certainly—certainly—I have thought a great deal about that. In fact, I—I—that is—well, my darling, I understood that old Mrs. Hetherington had been pressing about your staying in Haus Place. It is the London Season, you know.

MRS. JERMYN.

There can be no season anywhere for a wife without her husband.

SPENCER JERMYN.

My dear Diana, I am delighted to hear you say that. I *do* leave you a great deal—I *am* always flying here, there, and everywhere. It is wrong—it is damnably wrong!

MRS. JERMYN.

[*Holding her hands over* TINY's *ears.*] Spencer, the child!

SPENCER JERMYN.

Ugh! I beg *your* pardon, Diana—but confound that ugly child!

MRS. JERMYN.

Oh, no!

SPENCER JERMYN.

I repeat, it is wrong that I should go about in this way alone. Therefore let us remedy it.

MRS. JERMYN.

Willingly.

SPENCER JERMYN.

Ah, that's right, my darling.

MRS. JERMYN.

But I fear, Spencer, that you overestimate your powers of resolve in thinking that you can forego those dreadful race-meetings.

SPENCER JERMYN.

My dear Diana, I don't suggest that. I was about to propose that you accompany me.

MRS. JERMYN.

Spencer! Pray respect me a little!

[TINY *sits at the foot of a tree with a book.*]

SPENCER JERMYN.

Husbands and wives *are* seen together at these places.

MRS. JERMYN.

What grade of wife?

SPENCER JERMYN.

What grade of wife! Why, the—the.—the ordinary sort of married wife.

MRS. JERMYN.

Then I am not the ordinary sort of wife. I confess I may possess one faculty less than other women—that faculty is The Stable, the Stable in all its bearings and influences, public and private.

SPENCER JERMYN.

Diana, this is simple prejudice?

MRS. JERMYN.

What *is* a stable—your own stable, for which you so often leave me? It is the least comfortable part of our premises, where common men are always shouting "Get back," or "Come over," and carrying about pails of water!

SPENCER JERMYN.

It isn't the stable, Diana—it's the horses, the noble, intelligent horses.

MRS. JERMYN.

The only use you find for them is to drag you or carry you from one place to another.

SPENCER JERMYN.

Don't they do it well?

MRS. JERMYN.

Certainly—then let it end there. When a train

does the same thing in an eighth of the time you
don't pat the steam-engine and smoke pipes with
the railway directors. And then, these dreadful
festivals called The Races — the races, where you
put the very animal you profess to respect and admire to a speed it was never meant to attain, and
where your jockey lashes and wounds the beast he
rides because the poor thing is too fragile to "make
the pace," or too intelligent to risk breaking a
blood-vessel. The Races! A mere Bacchanal of
vulgarity and depravity, whose vice sinks into a
man until his very tongue becomes furred with it
and he can speak only in the shibboleth of the Bet-
ting Ring.

SPENCER JERMYN.

My dear, Sport is the natural wear of man, like
his coat and trousers—it is perfectly becoming that
a woman should not adopt the one or the other.

MRS. JERMYN.

Spencer!

SPENCER JERMYN.

The instinct of Sport is born in us. In all prob-
ability Adam had a gun license—and as there were
horses in Eden there you have the origin of Ascot.
It was the presence of Eve which made it a ladies'
meeting.

MRS. JERMYN.

Hush, Spencer—the child!

SPENCER JERMYN.

Racing is my hobby—my weakness, if you like.

Bless my soul and body, *you* have a hobby which *is* a weakness!

MRS. JERMYN.

And pray what is that, Spencer?

SPENCER JERMYN.

[*Pointing to* TINY.] There's an animated fraction of it over there. There are four or five more of them stabled—I beg your pardon, Diana—domiciled in our house at this moment. I don't bring my horses indoors.

MRS. JERMYN.

A few local orphans happen to be occupying the nursery. You know—you must be aware—that we have no other use for the nursery.

SPENCER JERMYN.

My dear Diana, if we *are* to argue let us argue respectfully and fairly!

MRS. JERMYN.

I admit, Spencer, that I *am* absorbingly interested in little boys. To wander freely through the courts and alleys of the most wretched districts of London, finding small human treasures amongst the flotsam and jetsam of the great metropolis, is the furthermost ambition my mind can grasp. [*Coaxingly.*] Promise me, Spencer, promise me that when the summer is gone and the chill misery of the wet winter is upon us, that you will spend a day with me in Poplar?

SPENCER JERMYN.

No, Diana, certainly not — any day in Bond Street——

MRS. JERMYN.

Oh, you are odious!

SPENCER JERMYN.

. Our own parish of Over-Lessingham contains enough poverty to satisfy any moderate philanthropist ; do what you like *here.*

MRS. JERMYN.

Spencer! You mean that? You give me permission to do what I please in Lessingham for the welfare of our poor people?

SPENCER JERMYN.

Certainly, my darling—and I was about to tell you of an idea of mine for enlarging your scheme of operations.

MRS. JERMYN.

Oh, you dear old darling! Sit down there! And I'll sit at your feet as I used to before we—before we——

SPENCER JERMYN.

Before we were philanthropists.

MRS. JERMYN.

Before we were married. And I'll give you back your old nick-name of " Nettles."

SPENCER JERMYN.

Thank you, Diana.

MRS. JERMYN.

[*Pinching his chin.*] Good-humoured, irritable, irritating old Nettles! And I'll tell you all about the great big plan I've had in my poor anxious head for weeks, and weeks, and weeks.

SPENCER JERMYN.

Do, my darling—and then you shall hear my proposition, which I fancy——

MRS. JERMYN.

Hush, Nettles, dear ; you do rattle on so.

SPENCER JERMYN.

I beg your pardon, my darling.

MRS. JERMYN.

Nettles, dear.

SPENCER JERMYN.

[*Affectionately.*] Yes, Diana.

MRS. JERMYN.

I don't believe we shall ever get a tenant for that farm-house at Shodly Heath.

SPENCER JERMYN.

Eh ?

MRS. JERMYN.

It has been vacant so long—why should we not ourselves turn it to account.

SPENCER JERMYN.

Well now, that's a little strange—the same notion had already struck me.

Mrs. Jermyn.

Oh, you dear old Nettles! I know! Nettles has been having what he calls "a good time of it" at that awful Epsom. And yet I'm not angry with him. Well then, dear, this is my plan—the children *are* in the way at Odlum House—in your way, I mean.

Spencer Jermyn.

They certainly are.

Mrs. Jermyn.

And when they all have the whooping cough it will be distressing to Nettle's ear. Now, why shouldn't we furnish the Shodly Heath farm——

Spencer Jermyn.

Diana!

Mrs. Jermyn.

Turn Mrs. Clegg, our old housekeeper, into a sort of Matron, and make the farm-house a Refuge for thirty or forty of my little waifs?

Spencer Jermyn.

My dear Diana, to a very great extent *my* plan is *yours.*

Mrs. Jermyn.

Oh!

Spencer Jermyn.

I had already determined to furnish the Farm for benevolent purposes——

Mrs. Jermyn.

Tiny—Tiny Landon! Come here!
[*The child runs across to her: she wipes his
nose.*]

Mrs. Jermyn.

Oh! you precious little charge! Tiny, kiss that
gentleman, and make, oh, so much of him!
[*She places the child on* Jermyn's *knee; he
struggles, and pushes* Tiny *from him.*]

Spencer Jermyn.

Diana, you will not let me explain. I certainly
have arranged that the Farm at Shodly shall be a
Home or Refuge—but, pardon me, Diana, not, *not*
for little boys.

Mrs. Jermyn.

What! Not—for—little—boys?

Spencer Jermyn.

No, Diana.

Mrs. Jermyn.

For little girls?

Spencer Jermyn.

No, Diana.

Mrs. Jermyn.

For whom then is Shodly to be a shelter?

Spencer Jermyn.

I thought it would satisfy and delight you, Diana
—twenty decayed jockeys.

MRS. JERMYN.

Oh!

[SHATTOCK *and* PEWS *lounge out of the house with pipes in their mouths.*]

SHATTOCK.

[*To* PEWS.] 'Ats off—the duchess!

MRS. JERMYN.

Are these two of them?

SPENCER JERMYN.

Samuel Shattock—a friend of his.

MRS. JERMYN.

They are indeed decayed.

SPENCER JERMYN.

Diana, remember they were—both of them—little boys once.

[PINCHING *and* MISS MOXON, *talking earnestly, come out of the house.*]

SPENCER JERMYN.

[*Angrily to* SHATTOCK *and* PEWS.] Do try to make a favourable impression upon the ladies, please! Put those pipes away.

[*They touch their hats and tap the contents of their pipes against the heels of their boots.*]

MISS MOXON.

[*Quietly to* MRS. JERMYN.] Diana, I'm almost a happy woman.

c

Mrs. JERMYN.

I'm quite a wretched one.

Miss MOXON.

I really think Ralph Pinching is in love with me. [*Miss Moxon walks away ecstatically,* PINCHING *looking after her.*]

SPENCER JERMYN.

Oh, Pinching, I want you to enter into my scheme with Mrs. Jermyn. [*Quietly.*] Be sanguine about it. [PINCHING *pays no attention.*] Pinching!

PINCHING.

Eh? Oh, yes. [*Taking* JERMYN'S *arm.*] Jermyn, Miss Moxon's father was a captain in the Lancers.

SPENCER JERMYN.

Yes, yes, my boy. [PINCHING *joins* MISS MOXON *and begins talking earnestly.*] I wish to goodness Pinching would be more professional! Pinching, Pinching, my boy! Mrs. Jermyn wants to hear your notions about the Home.

PINCHING.

[*Carelessly.*] Eh? Oh, yes—great fun.

SPENCER JERMYN.

Mr. Pinching, I claim your attention for a few minutes, please.

PINCHING.

Certainly.

SPENCER JERMYN.

[*Pointing to a rustic table.*] There are pen, ink, and paper. [PINCHING *whispers to* MISS MOXON, *then seats himself at the table. She takes a chair by his side and they continue talking.*] Diana, pray sit down.

   [*As she is about to sit* SHATTOCK *hurries forward and dusts the seat with his handkerchief.*]

SHATTOCK.

One moment, lady—there, lady.

MRS. JERMYN.

[*Shrinking from him.*] Thank you!
       [*She sits with* TINY *by her side.*]

SHATTOCK.

The more I look at you, lady, the more I see the likeness to my poor missus. [*Pointing to* MRS. JERMYN.] Do you catch it, Edward?

PEWS.

Striking—to your *fust* missus.

SHATTOCK.

What do you mean, goin' on like that?

PEWS.

I mean the missus you had when I fust knew you, Sam.

SPENCER JERMYN.

Hush, hush, hush! Diana, my dear, I want you to understand—and so does Mr. Pinching— [*To*

PINCHING, *who is engaged with* MISS MOXON.] Pinching!—that all the thoughtfulness, all the charity of
this notion has been animated by your beautiful,
your magnificent example in dealing with little
boys. That child is tearing your gown, Diana;
box his ears—box his ears! But, Diana, as Pinching aptly reminds us—Pinching, please!—as Pinching reminds us, the world is not exclusively peopled
by little boys.

MRS. JERMYN.

Is it peopled with anything more innocent, more
precious than little boys? .

SPENCER JERMYN.

H'm! No, my dear—but you oughtn't to con-
centrate innocence on Shodly Heath; you ought to
diffuse it. Now, men like Mr. Shattock—step a
little forward, Shattock; my wife can't see you well
—men like Mr. Shattock are victims of lost oppor-
tunities.

SHATTOCK.

True, lady.

SPENCER JERMYN.

Mr. Shattock was once a jockey of considerable
promise.

SHATTOCK.

I was brought low, lady, by being got at by the
wealthy and unscrup'lous. Whenever I had a good
mount, lady, and stood a chance of being in the one-
two-three, I was always got at, lady. Examine the
knuckle—muscles of that 'and, lady. [MRS. JERMYN

shrinks back.] You may take my 'and in yours, lady. That 'and is developed through pullin'—pullin' 'ard.

MRS. JERMYN.

What do you mean, man?

SHATTOCK.

Pullin' a 'orse's 'ead when he was a' doin' too well, lady—ridin' for to lose. Ah, lady, there's many a good 'orse wot Sam Shattock has rode wot had tooth-ache in his back teeth for years followin'. And see the hend of it! Those there 'orses have come to cabs and me to a 'ome on Shodly 'Eath. And it's a moral lesson, I say, and proud I am to preach it.

SPENCER JERMYN.

You see, Diana, we have found some good here, I venture to think.

MRS. JERMYN.

At least you have developed an extraordinary talent for discovery. I wonder how it will strike Mr. Pilkington, the vicar.

SPENCER JERMYN.

Oh, I've a fine plan for managing Pilkington.

MRS. JERMYN.

Have you? His poor wife would be glad to know it.

SPENCER JERMYN.

I shall conciliate Pilkington by appointing a sal-aried warden.

MRS. JERMYN.

Not a clergyman!

SPENCER JERMYN.

Certainly.

PEWS.

[*To himself.*] Oh, crikey!

SPENCER JERMYN.

A young liberal-minded sporting parson.

MRS. JERMYN.

[*Impatiently.*] Oh!

SHATTOCK.

Here, mister! I sha'n't never get no twenty men to the post if a parson's going to hold the flag!

SPENCER JERMYN.

Silence! I have never met so much senseless opposition!

SHATTOCK.

Here, mister——

SPENCER JERMYN.

Shattock and Pews, you can go!

SHATTOCK.

[*To* MRS. JERMYN.] Speak for us, lady—don't let 'im get his 'ead in this 'ere. Pull 'im, lady, pull 'im! Oh! here's another element crep' in!

[SHATTOCK *and* PEWS *take their leave.*]

SPENCER JERMYN.

One would think I was a little boy—no, by Jove, I should be better treated if I were. Pinching! Mr. Pinching! Miss Moxon, please—really!

PINCHING.

[*Snatching up a pen and arranging a sheet of paper.*] I'm waiting for you, Jermyn.

SPENCER JERMYN.

The advertisement for the clerical papers.

MRS. JERMYN.

Ha!   [*She sends* TINY *away.*]

SPENCER JERMYN.

[*Dictating.*] "Shodly Heath Home."

MRS. JERMYN.

Ha! ha! ha! After all my plans!

SPENCER JERMYN.

[*Resuming.*] "Opportunity for a Young Church-man in sympathy with our National Sports and Pastimes."

MRS. JERMYN.

There is no such man in existence!

SPENCER JERMYN.

Then there ought to be! "The Founder"—[MISS MOXON *and* PINCHING *are talking again.*] Pinching— Miss Moxon—upon my word, I— "The Founder desires the co-operation, as Warden, of an open-minded, unprejudiced——"

MRS. JERMYN.

Ha! ha!

SPENCER JERMYN.

Mr. Pinching, will you oblige me by following me into the house with your papers. Diana, your behaviour pains and vexes me!

[*He ascends the steps and disappears through the porch.* PINCHING *follows with the writing materials.*]

MISS MOXON.

[*Following* PINCHING.] Is this then to be our good-bye?

PINCHING.

I'm very sorry to have to run away. You won't think me rude, will you? Do leave your address.

SPENCER JERMYN.

[*Returning.*] Mr. Pinching!

PINCHING.

[*To* MISS MOXON.] Excuse me!
[*He follows* JERMYN *hastily into the house.*]

MISS MOXON.

Leave my address! What an end to everything! Leave my address! It's abominable! One would think Mr. Jermyn did it on purpose to spoil my prospects!

MRS. JERMYN.

Mr. Jermyn would do anything to spoil anybody's prospects—mine particularly.

MISS MOXON.

I ask, how is it possible for a woman to get married?

MRS. JERMYN.

Would it were not possible! A woman's only chance of happiness is in remaining single.

MISS MOXON.

I *quite* agree with you; but I shouldn't mind being wretched with Mr. Pinching.

MRS. JERMYN.

I can't talk to you about Mr. Pinching, Constance; I can't talk or think of anything but the blow which has fallen upon me.

MISS MOXON.

Don't consider me unsympathetic, Diana, but I can't talk to you about your blow. To think that he sat upon this very seat and with the words, " Constance, my darling," in his heart was set to draw up an advertisement!

MRS. JERMYN.

To think that this is the end of all my dreams for the last few weeks, day and night! This is the end of my pleasant picture of forty babbling babies rolling upon the grass at Shodly, filling the diamond casements of the farm-house with their fresh, ruddy faces, or making its old rooms ring with the rattle of their metal spoons! Oh!

Miss Moxon.

At the very moment of my life when I am not getting younger! At the very instant I am starting to London, to a nasty humiliating situation! It's not giving him a chance, poor fellow!

Mrs. Jermyn.

My little boys! My poor little boys!

Miss Moxon.

But this is a grown-up man!

Mrs. Jermyn.

Ah, you don't worship little children.

Miss Moxon.

I could—I want to—but not so much other people's.

Mrs. Jermyn.

The home I could make for them!

Miss Moxon.

The home I could make for *him!* [*Sitting distractedly upon the steps.*] Oh, let people come and trample on me—I don't care.

Mrs. Jermyn.

Constance, dear, don't—Mr. Pinching may write to you.

Miss Moxon.

No—he's a lawyer. He naturally wouldn't commit his views to paper.

Mrs. Jermyn.

Then why not delay your journey to London ?

Miss Moxon.

That's impossible. I gave my word a month ago that I would go to Mr. Brice this week at latest, and to-day is the last day of the week, and the twelve-fifteen is the only train to get me there by tea-time.

Mrs. Jermyn.

Mr. Brice ! Who and what is Mr. Brice ?

Miss Moxon.

I've never seen him ; he is the curate of the very poorest parish in London—St. Jacob's-in-the-East ; that's all I know.

Mrs. Jermyn.

[*Ecstatically.*] The poorest parish in London !

Miss Moxon.

Mr. Brice has met with some accident and is going away for a holiday, and I am to look after his niece in his absence and help with the horrid district visiting.

Mrs. Jermyn.

Help with the horrid district visiting ! Oh, how glorious ! how beautiful !

Miss Moxon.

How hateful! how odious!

Mrs. Jermyn.

To you comes the opportunity that is denied to me and you despise it. St. Jacob's-in-the-East! The East, the very Mecca of the pilgrimage I have dreamed of! Oh, if I could but be in your place!

Miss Moxon.

Diana!

Mrs. Jermyn.

Well?

Miss Moxon.

Diana! Would you like to be in my place *really?*

Mrs. Jermyn.

Constance!

Miss Moxon.

This Mr. Brice doesn't know me, has never seen me. I answered his advertisement in the *Seraphim* when I was in London and he didn't even trouble to take up my references. He expects a Miss Moxon to-day not later than four o'clock; that's all. If you desperately wish it, why shouldn't you be Miss Moxon for two or three weeks?

Mrs. Jermyn.

Oh! Mr. Jermyn would never allow it.

Miss Moxon.

He will not be here. When he returns, you have been visiting; there's the explanation.

MRS. JERMYN.

The children in the nursery!

MISS MOXON.

Leave me to look after the little darlings.

MRS. JERMYN.

Oh, Connie, I dare not play such a trick!

MISS MOXON.

Ah, when you were courting I helped you!

MRS. JERMYN.

Besides, you forget everything; how can I travel to town in the train with Spencer?

MISS MOXON.

I never thought of that. Oh, Ralph, Ralph, why didn't you speak when you had the opportunity! I know! Di! I can get you to town by the twelve-fifteen.

MRS. JERMYN.

Be quiet, Constance. Who would take me to the station?

MISS MOXON.

Your husband!

MRS. JERMYN.

He would know I'm not going visiting without any luggage!

MISS MOXON.

He shan't know you're going to town to-day at all.

MRS. JERMYN.

You're quite mad, Constance.

MISS MOXON.

Never was saner in my life.
  [*The voices of* JERMYN *and* PINCHING *are heard within.*]

SPENCER JERMYN.

[*In the house.*]   Make a careful copy of it, Pinching.

MISS MOXON.

Your husband and my Pinching! Go indoors and wait till I come.

[PINCHING *and* JERMYN *come from the house, the latter dressed for travelling.*]

MRS. JERMYN.

[*To* MISS MOXON.]   Constance, mind! I can't—I won't.

SPENCER JERMYN.

Good-bye, Diana! I feel sure you will have grown to like my plans for the Shodly Heath Home by the time I get back. We—we part affectionately I hope, Diana?

MRS. JERMYN.

Certainly, Spencer.

SPENCER JERMYN.

Good-bye, dear!

MRS. JERMYN.

Good-bye!   [*They shake hands.*

SPENCER JERMYN.

[*With assumed heartiness.*] Good-bye, my darling! Don't sit in any draughts. Good-bye!
[MRS. JERMYN *turns away.*]

SPENCER JERMYN.

My dear Miss Moxon, you will never be ready to drive with me to the station.

MISS MOXON.

Oh, thank you, Mr. Jermyn, but my arrangements are altered—Diana has persuaded me not to go to-day.

MRS. JERMYN.

[*In an undertone.*] Constance!

SPENCER JERMYN.

I'm very glad.

MISS MOXON.

But there is somebody I want you to take with you to the station ; not in the carriage, of course— let her ride on the box with Gibbs. Will you?

SPENCER JERMYN.

Certainly. Who is it?

MISS MOXON.

Poor Mrs. Landon, who is obliged to go to London on business.

MRS. JERMYN.

[*Under her breath.*] Oh!
[*She runs into the house.*]

SPENCER JERMYN.

Diana's run away! Ah! poor Diana.

MISS MOXON.

I'll go after her.

[*She follows* MRS. JERMYN *into the house.*]

PINCHING.

You'll telegraph to me, Jermyn, from time to time in case I should want to get at you suddenly, won't you?

SPENCER JERMYN.

Yes; but, Pinching, do you know that I've half a mind to let the Steeplechase and the Grand Prix go to the devil and stop at home? Diana—disappointed, poor girl; and lonely, eh, Pinching?

PINCHING.

Well, Miss Moxon remains a little longer, and then there are the children.

SPENCER JERMYN.

That's true. Confound those children!

[HEWETT *enters.*]

HEWETT.

Gibbs has taken the carriage round, sir.

SPENCER JERMYN.

All right. Tell them I'm waiting. [HEWETT *goes into the house.*] Good-bye, Pinching. It doesn't strike you that I am a bad husband to Diana, does it? A brute—does it, Pinching, eh?

PINCHING.

My dear Jermyn! Don't think of such a thing.

SPENCER JERMYN.

Poor Diana.

[*HEWETT comes out of the house carrying a travelling bag and rug.*]

HEWETT.

Have to look sharp to catch the twelve-fifteen, sir.

SPENCER. JERMYN.

Of course—of course. Where is that Mrs. Landon? Mrs. Landon! Mrs. Landon!

[*MISS MOXON enters from the house, followed by MRS. JERMYN in MRS. LANDON's black shawl and bonnet and veil.*]

SPENCER JERMYN.

[*Testily.*] Come along, Mrs. Landon, come along. [*Turning to PINCHING.*] Remember, Pinching——
[*He speaks in an undertone to PINCHING.*]

MISS MOXON.

[*To MRS. JERMYN, giving her an envelope.*] The Reverend Noel Brice, Number Eight Pelican Place, Great Raggatt Street, East. I'll send your luggage off to-night.

MRS. JERMYN.

Oh!

SPENCER JERMYN.

But where's Diana? Surely she'll walk with me to the gate?

E

Miss Moxon.

Oh—I—she——

Spencer Jermyn.

I won't leave her like this. Confound the train! I'll go back and kiss her!

Miss Moxon.

Ah! Mr. Jermyn, she's in the nursery with the boys.

Spencer Jermyn.

Oh, the deuce! Say I left my love. Look sharp, Hewett!
[JERMYN *goes away, followed by* HEWETT, MRS. JERMYN *hurrying after them.* PINCHING *detains* MISS MOXON.]

Pinching.

Miss Moxon, I shall be here—on business—to-morrow at eleven o'clock. May I see you?

Miss Moxon.

[*About to follow* MRS. JERMYN.] Oh, indeed you may, Mr. Pinching.

Pinching.

I wish to ask you a question which concerns my happiness. I—I—— What's the matter?
[MISS MOXON *gives a slight scream and waves her hands toward the house as if to keep someone from coming out.*]

MISS MOXON.

No, no—not yet!

[MRS. LANDON, *without a bonnet or shawl, runs from the house looking about her.*]

PINCHING.

Mrs. Landon!

MRS. LANDON.

Where's my boy? I can't find my Tiny anywhere. [*She hurries away.*]

PINCHING.

Good gracious! Isn't that Widow Landon? Why, Jermyn thinks she's riding on the box-seat. Jermyn!

MISS MOXON.

[*Obstructing his way.*] No, no, Mr. Pinching; don't, don't!

PINCHING.

[*Trying to pass her.*] Excuse me, Miss Moxon; Jermyn ought to know of this! Jermyn!
   [*He passes* MISS MOXON ; *she clings to him.*]

MISS MOXON.

No, no, Mr. Pinching! I—I'll tell you something.

PINCHING.

I'll be back in a moment.

Miss Moxon.

No, you mustn't! What shall I do? Mr. Pinching! I—I—I love you, Mr. Pinching!

Pinching.

Oh, my dear Miss Moxon!
[*They sink on to the garden-seat side by side.*]

.

END OF THE FIRST ACT.

THE SECOND ACT.

A CHAPTER OF SENTIMENT.

The scene is two rather commonly furnished sitting-rooms, separated by folding-doors, in a dull, som-·bre lodging-house in the East End of London. Through the back windows is seen a large gloomy church. It is the dwelling-place of the REV. NOEL BRICE.

The REV. NOEL BRICE, *a pale, careworn-looking young man, is writing at a table, with his wrist bound up, while his niece,* BERTHA, *a pretty girl of about six-teen, is seen through the folding-doors making tea in the further room.*

NOEL BRICE.

[*As he writes.*] "Now the question you must ask yourselves is, What is philanthropy? Because if it be not a mere nickname for some crazy idiosyn-crasy of the rich there is no reason why you poor people should not be true philanthropists." [*He leans back wearily.*] How this wretched wrist throbs, to be sure.

[BERTHA *comes from the further room.*]

BERTHA.

Uncle Noel, isn't Tom—isn't Mr. Clark coming down-stairs to drink tea with us this evening?

NOEL BRICE.

[*Resuming writing.*] I don't know, Bertha, dear. We can't expect the boy to be always gossiping here.

BERTHA.

[*To herself.*] But he said my tea was the best in the world. It doesn't sound like a thing a man would say if he didn't mean it. [*To* NOEL.] How many sermons for Sunday, Uncle Noel?

NOEL BRICE.

Two. Dr. Porcher is too unwell to preach.

BERTHA.

Which are you working at now?

NOEL BRICE.

The second.

BERTHA.

Oh, then you're nearly finished.

NOEL BRICE.

No, dear—I always begin with the second.

BERTHA.

Rest your hand a little while and let me be your amanuensis.

NOEL BRICE.

No, thank you, ladybird, I'll wait till Miss Moxon comes in.

BERTHA.

[*To herself.*] He never lets me help him, and I'm his niece. Why does he like dictating to Miss Moxon and not to me? He has only known her about nine or ten days and she is no relation at all.

[MRS. JERMYN *enters in walking costume.*]

BERTHA.

Here's Miss Moxon, Noel.

MRS. JERMYN.

[*Kissing* BERTHA.] Have I been out a very long time?

NOEL BRICE.

It seems so. Where have you been doing good this afternoon?

MRS. JERMYN.

Nowhere. I have been attempting to visit Tyke's Court.

NOEL BRICE.

Not alone?

MRS. JERMYN.

No. I met the young gentleman who lodges upstairs, Mr. Clark, and he went with me.

BERTHA.

[*To herself.*] My Tom.

NOEL BRICE.

And what is your opinion of Tyke's Court?

MRS. JERMYN.

It is an unsavoury locality, which will see me no more. I cry beaten, Mr. Brice—I have failed again to-day.

NOEL BRICE.

Failed—in what, Miss Moxon?

MRS. JERMYN.

Failed to come up to my own aspirations. For days and days I have peered in at the opening of Tyke's Court and felt it my duty to tread a path through its decomposed cabbage-leaves. I have made innumerable cowardly excuses—one day I have not felt well ; another, I had left my camphor at home, and so on. This afternoon I plunged. Oh ! the horror of it ! "Are you going to faint ? " Mr. Clark asked me. "I think so," I whispered ; "get me out—only get me out ! " He got me out, and I sat down in a chemist's.

NOEL BRICE.

Ah, visiting Tyke's Court is man's work.

MRS. JERMYN.

No, not even man's work. Tyke's Court ought to be visited and consoled by machinery. Oh, the men and the women ! I don't know which were which, but Mr. Clark assures me I saw both.

BERTHA.

Didn't you discover any children?

MRS. JERMYN.

Mr. Clark said I did. There were some objects smaller than others—those, I understand, were the children.

BERTHA.

When you first came to us, Miss Moxon, you were going to fondle all the little ones in our parish.

MRS. JERMYN.

Oh, so I would! So I would, to-morrow—now—*if* somebody would only wash them!

NOEL BRICE.

[*Writing again.*] Ah, we shall get them washed in time.

MRS. JERMYN.

In time! [*To herself.*] And I'm going home in a few days.

BERTHA.

There's a letter for you, Miss Moxon, on the mantelpiece.

MRS. JERMYN.

[*Rising and taking the letter.*] Oh, thank you.

BERTHA.

[*Quietly to her.*] Did Mr. Clark happen to say he was coming down-stairs this evening—to see Uncle Noel?

Mrs. Jermyn.

Yes, he is coming— [*Kissing her.*] to see Uncle Noel.

[BERTHA *runs into the further room and goes out.*
Mrs. JERMYN *opens her letter.*]

Mrs. Jermyn.

[*To herself.*] From Constance! Her letters make me tremble. [*Reading.*] " Dear Di. I grow more horribly nervous about our escapade every day. I get absolutely no consolation from Mr. Pinching. Of course, after his discovery of Mrs. Landon, I was forced to admit that you had gone away on a Philanthropic Mission ; but I refused to disclose your whereabouts, and his kisses are but on the brow." Poor Constance ; for my sake ! " The servants gossiped so at your sudden disappearance that I thought it best to tip them lavishly all round—therefore, Mrs. Clegg, the housekeeper, has your new Indian shawl. No news of Mr. Jermyn beyond the Paris letter which I sent you, but Mr. Pinching went to London yesterday, and I can't get rid of the impression that he has an appointment with your husband in town." Oh ! how near ; perhaps this very day, too ! " Now, if Mr. Jermyn should return here prematurely what *am* I to say ? I think I shall feign madness and babble incoherently. Dear Diana, *do* come home ! The blot which follows is a tear. Your engagement—I mean my engagement—I mean *our* engagement with Mr. Brice was merely as companion to his niece during his holiday. When do you expect him back ? " [*Looking at* NOEL.] When do I expect him back ? He won't start, poor fel-

low ! " Get him home by all means ; no man, no
curate at any rate, ever needs more than ten days'
rest, and you have been absent that time from your
distracted—Constance Moxon. P.S.—I pulled a gray
hair from my head this morning. N.B.—About
a dozen awful men have taken up their abode at
Shodly Heath Farm. We close all our shutters
now." [*Putting the letter in her pocket.*] Oh, yes, I
must extricate myself from this predicament to-morrow—the next day, at latest. What should keep
me at St. Jacob's when I have failed so miserably in
the work I thought my true mission ? [BERTHA *returns to the inner room and busies herself with the
tea-things.*] But why hasn't Mr. Brice gone for his
holiday? I can't make that out at all. [NOEL *is
thinking, pen in hand ; she approaches the writing-
table.*] Mr. Brice.

NOEL BRICE.

[*Starting.*] Miss Moxon.

MRS. JERMYN.

Mr. Brice, have you forgotten why you engaged
me—er—why you engaged a companion for your
niece ?

NOEL BRICE.

No—let me see. I wanted a lady to do some of
the easy visiting and to keep Bertha company while
I——

MRS. JERMYN.

While you were absent from London on your
holiday.

NOEL BRICE.

Oh, yes—I was going away, wasn't I?

MRS. JERMYN.

You were—and aren't you?

NOEL BRICE.

Not now—I've changed my mind.

MRS. JERMYN.

Changed your mind!

NOEL BRICE.

The fact is, the rector and I don't agree very well, or, rather, Mrs. Porcher, his wife, doesn't like me—and Mrs. Porcher *is* the rector, and both the churchwardens of St. Jacob's. She was very angry at the idea of my wanting rest, and besides — besides, when *you* came I felt as if I no longer needed a holiday.

MRS. JERMYN.

I am afraid, Mr. Brice, I want to ask you now to let me—to let me—go.

NOEL BRICE.

Let you go! Let you leave us, Miss Moxon?

MRS. JERMYN.

To-morrow.

NOEL BRICE.

So soon!

MRS. JERMYN.

Or next day. Your niece no longer needs a companion, and I have failed wretchedly in my visiting, and—and I have other reasons.

NOEL BRICE.

I am very sorry.

MRS. JERMYN.

Thank you. Dear Bertha will miss me.

NOEL BRICE.

Miss you ! Ah, so much.

MRS. JERMYN.

And it is concerning Bertha that I want to leave a little warning behind me. Mr. Brice, who and what is this Mr. Clark ?

NOEL BRICE.

You don't dislike him ?

MRS. JERMYN.

Oh, I like him very much.

NOEL BRICE.

So do I, and that's nearly all I know—that I like him. You see this sprained wrist ? Well, that might have taken the form of a broken head or a broken back but for Tom Clark.

MRS. JERMYN.

A hero !

NOEL BRICE.

No, a typical English lad. I interfered one night in a drunken riot down below here, near the docks. Clark came to my aid and we fought our way out of it, back to back. He had just come ashore from a voyage—he's a sailor, you know—so I got him a lodging upstairs, in this house—and we're friends. That's Tom Clark.

MRS. JERMYN.

Thank you, Mr. Brice. Now don't you think you had better find out something more about the boy as soon as possible?

NOEL BRICE.

Why?

MRS. JERMYN.

Why, in case he should fall in love with Bertha.

NOEL BRICE.

Fall in love!

MRS. JERMYN.

Don't men fall in love, Mr. Brice?

NOEL BRICE.

[*Looking at her earnestly.*] I beg your pardon— yes, indeed.   [*There is a knock at the door.*]

TOM CLARK.

[*Speaking outside.*] Will somebody open the door?

NOEL BRICE.

There is the boy. [*Opening the door to admit* TOM CLARK, *a bright young fellow of about twenty, with a breezy, impulsive manner, who carries a large card-board box.*] What have you got there, Tom?

TOM CLARK.

I don't know—dynamite, I think. The carrier left it at the door as I came down. [*To* MRS. JERMYN.] I hope you're better.

MRS. JERMYN.

Very much, thank you.

TOM CLARK.

Oh, Miss Moxon was such fun at the chemist's.

BERTHA.

[*Coming from the other room.*] A box!

TOM CLARK.

Addressed to "The Curate of St. Jacob's-in-the-East."

NOEL BRICE.

Some response to our appeal for the poor children, I expect.

BERTHA and MRS. JERMYN.

[*Delighted.*] Oh!

NOEL BRICE.

Open it for them, Tom.

[*He goes into the further room and takes up a newspaper.* TOM *worries at the string of the box, while the two women look on eagerly.*]

TOM CLARK.

I wonder what is inside—guess.

BERTHA.

I know—little white frocks.

MRS. JERMYN.

No, Bertha, surely not—brown frocks with small holland aprons are more serviceable.

TOM CLARK.

It's very securely done up.

BERTHA.

If it's frocks, there must be at least twenty.

MRS. JERMYN.

It must be frocks; the appeal was so piteously worded.

BERTHA.

Make haste, Tom—it might be boots.

MRS. JERMYN.

Of course it is—it's boots!

BERTHA.

That's it—it's boots!

MRS. JERMYN and BERTHA.

Boots, boots, boots!

TOM CLARK.

[*Hot with his exertion.*] That's it!
[*He takes the lid from the box and puts his hand inside.*]

BERTHA.

What is it, Tom? It isn't frocks.

MRS. JERMYN.

Nor boots.

TOM CLARK.

Here's a list on the top. [*Producing an open sheet of note-paper.*] A gold crest!

MRS. JERMYN and BERTHA.

Oh!

TOM CLARK.

[*Reading.*] "Portman Square. Mrs. Horace W. Pigott-Blundell, in response to the affecting appeal in to-day's paper, has pleasure in forwarding to the curate of St. Jacob's-in-the-East, for distribution among the deserving, thirty numbers of the *Illustrated London News.*" [*He throws the letter into the box and bangs the lid on it in disgust, saying to himself.*] And I paid one and eightpence for the carriage! [*He carries the box into the further room, followed by* BERTHA.]

MRS. JERMYN.

[*Sitting at the writing-table.*] Mr. Brice's sermon. [*Reading.*] "What is philanthropy?" Ah, what is it? Is it that bundle of picture papers, or Spencer's wretched freak at Shodly, or my foolish deceit in taking Constance's place here? Shall I ever find out?

[TOM *comes to* MRS. JERMYN.]

TOM CLARK.

Miss Moxon, are you inclined to help a fellow?

E

Mrs. Jermyn.

What fellow, Mr. Clark?

Tom Clark.

Look here! I like you, Miss Moxon. I think you're a brick, and I know you have a jolly lot of influence with Noel—Mr. Brice.

Mrs. Jermyn.

I!

Tom Clark.

Yes, rather. And I want you to use it for me like a dear good soul. Will you?

Mrs. Jermyn.

How?

Tom Clark.

In this way. [Bertha *comes from the further room carrying a cup of tea in each hand, but stops short when she hears her name mentioned.*] I'm in love with Bertha! I love her fearfully! Nobody suspects it, because I'm so careful. But she's going shopping after tea and I'm to escort her—and I know she'll take my arm.

Mrs. Jermyn.

She won't if you don't ask her.

Tom Clark.

But I feel I *shall* ask her. I say to myself, "I love Bertha," all day long—I go to sleep with the

words on my tongue—I wake up with them there—
they're there now. And when I talk to her as we
trudge along the streets together I shall be obliged
to open my mouth and out they'll roll—won't they?

[BERTHA *returns solemnly on tiptoe to the further
room, carrying the cups.*]

BERTHA.

[*In a whisper.*] I won't interrupt them just now.

MRS. JERMYN.

It seems to me that you don't want much assistance, Mr. Clark.

TOM CLARK.

But I shall, to get Noel's consent to our marriage;
because I want to be married at once.

MRS. JERMYN.

Oh! Would next week do?

TOM CLARK.

Yes, next week would do very well, thank you.
As far as I'm concerned I could wait a week longer,
but I'm not selfish altogether, Miss Moxon, and I'm
burning to help old Noel.

MRS. JERMYN.

But I don't see how——

TOM CLARK.

Why, Noel is awfully poor, driven like a slave,

worked to death. Ah, you don't guess what a fine
chap he is.

[*They both turn to look into the further room.*
BERTHA *is talking to* NOEL, *who is stroking her
hair fondly.*]

TOM CLARK.

Poor fellow!

MRS. JERMYN.

Poor fellow!

TOM CLARK.

You know, when his brother died Noel took all
the children. Bertha's grown up, but there are
three very small ones with a nurse. And he gets a
hundred and twenty a year from old Porcher.

MRS. JERMYN.

Oh!

TOM CLARK.

Too much, isn't it? Well then, when I marry my
Bertha I shall get him out of the grinding grip of
old Mrs. Porcher and whip him off into the country,
where he'll pick up his strength in a jiffy. See?

MRS. JERMYN.

Oh, are you very well off, then?

TOM CLARK.

Haven't a brass button, you know.

MRS. JERMYN.

Really, Mr. Clark!

TOM CLARK.

But my dear old father is rich. He and I quarrel awfully.

MRS. JERMYN.

Well, then, how——

TOM CLARK.

Why, the moment I marry I write and break it gently to the dad—"Dear Dad, I'm married. Yours, *et cetera!* " See?

MRS. JERMYN.

Perfectly. That couldn't be a shock to him, could it?

TOM CLARK.

No. Well, then, what's the result? Dad burning with anxiety to see my wife—*my wife!* Oh, doesn't it sound jolly?

MRS. JERMYN.

It *sounds* pretty well!

TOM CLARK.

I take her home! I can picture father standing, glum and sulky, at the gate! "Who's this?" I can hear him saying it. "My wife, dad!" "Your wife! What, that pretty little fairy! I like your taste, my boy—come in, we dine at seven." See?

MRS. JERMYN.

You seem to have thought out everything very carefully.

Tom Clark.

Yes ; if every fellow were as cautious there wouldn't be so many injudicious marriages.

Noel Brice.

[*At the folding-doors.*] Tom, why don't you let Miss Moxon have some tea? What are you discussing?

Bertha.

[*Pulling* Noel *back.*] Oh, uncle, don't disturb them!

Tom Clark.

Just coming, Noel. [*To* Mrs. Jermyn.] Be quick. I see you'll help a fellow ; won't you, eh? Won't you?

Mrs. Jermyn.

[*To herself.*] Would this be philanthropy, I wonder? But, my dear Mr. Clark, if you are so certain of Bertha's influence, why not gain your father's consent before your marriage?

Tom Clark.

Ho! ho! you don't know my dad! When Bertha and I are married we'll ask you down. He's great fun. Besides, I've got a horrid stepmother. I know the kind of woman—thin, pale lady with spectacles, black hair falling down like window-curtains over her forehead—awful.

Noel Brice.

The tea is quite cold!

BERTHA.

[*Taking him away.*] Oh, no, it isn't—not quite.

MRS. JERMYN.

I'm coming.

TOM CLARK.

[*Seizing her hand as she is going into the further room.*] Miss Moxon! Oh, do get me married quickly ! Miss Moxon !

MRS. JERMYN.

Well, well, I'll think of what I can do

TOM CLARK.

Bless you for that, because you can do everything ! Ah, you're as good and as beautiful in your way as Bertha is in hers, and whenever a man falls in love with you, Miss Moxon, I hope he'll worship you as I worship my dear girl !

MRS. JERMYN.

Oh, no ! Please don't say that !

[MRS. JERMYN *goes into the further room to the tea-table as* BERTHA *with her hat on joins* TOM.]

BERTHA.

I'm ready, Mr. Clark. It seems selfish of me to drag you out.

TOM CLARK.

Not at all. Are we going far ?

BERTHA.

No—only just round the corner, to a hat-shop.

TOM CLARK.

Oh, don't you know any distant hat-shop.

BERTHA.

Yes, but I always deal at this particular one.

[NOEL *comes from the other room reading a newspaper.*]

BERTHA.

[*At the door.*]   Good-bye, Uncle Noel—I sha'n't be long.

NOEL BRICE.

Good-bye, dear.

TOM CLARK.

[*Softly.*]   Oh, Bertha, don't, don't say you won't be long !

BERTHA.

Mr. Clark !

TOM CLARK.

If you only knew—if you only guessed——

BERTHA.

Guessed what?

TOM CLARK.

How much I—how much I—want you to give the other hat-shops a chance !

[TOM *and* BERTHA *go from the room.*]

NOEL BRICE.

[*To himself.*]   Now.   Half a sermon from two leaves one and a half.   One sermon and a half between this and Sunday, my article to finish for

The Seraphim, a Mothers' Tea on Friday night, two dockyard carpenters, both very bad characters, to marry to-morrow morning. [*Sitting at the table.*] Come, Brice, my good fellow, you must put on the steam.

[MRS. JERMYN *approaches him, carrying a cup of tea.*]

MRS. JERMYN.

Am I not to write for you this evening, Mr. Brice?

NOEL BRICE.

Thank you, Miss Moxon; my wrist is good for another hour.

[*He writes busily, she stands watching him.*]

MRS. JERMYN.

[*To herself, watching* NOEL.] Poor fellow—poor, generous, warm-hearted fellow! Tired out, domineered over by Mrs. Porcher, a hundred and twenty a year cked out by a few articles for *The Seraphim*, and four orphan children to feed and nurture. Poor fellow!

NOEL BRICE.

[*Reading from sheet of his sermon.*] "It is true philanthropy to treat all mankind alike—not to turn your back upon any object because it does not belong to the particular class you have made it your habit or your boast to serve."

[*He resumes writing.*]

MRS. JERMYN.

[*To herself.*] Surely that applies to me. Oh, if I could only render this man some service!

Wouldn't *that* be real charity! I've never done anything half as good as that would be.

NOEL BRICE.

[*Dropping his pen and putting his hand to his wrist.*] Hallo, another twinge!

MRS. JERMYN.

Now, perhaps you will resign that chair, Mr. Brice.

NOEL BRICE.

Thank you. I fear I must.
[*He puts her in his place, then picks up the newspaper and glances at the advertisements.*]

MRS. JERMYN.

[*To herself.*] What could I do for him—what could I do? I can't think. Shall we begin work, Mr. Brice?

NOEL BRICE.

[*Without looking up from the newspaper.*] Please. Good gracious, I've never read anything so monstrous! Look here! "Shodly Heath Home for Decayed Jockeys!"

MRS. JERMYN.

Oh!

NOEL BRICE.

[*Reading.*] "Opportunity for a Young Churchman in sympathy with our National Sports and Pastimes." Upon my word!

MRS. JERMYN.

Perhaps it means—cricket.

NOEL BRICE.

Cricket! [*Resuming.*] "The Founder desires the co-operation, as Warden, of an open-minded, unprejudiced Evangelist who detects an elevating tendency in Horse Racing and who is prepared to maintain that the English Race-meeting is both harmless and exhilarating." Why the Founder ought to be kicked!

MRS. JERMYN.

No, he oughtn't. Why?

NOEL BRICE.

Why! Look here! "Three hundred pounds a year." Three hundred pounds a year! "Write to Ralph Pinching, Solicitor, High Street, Newmarket." There's a temptation, a gross temptation, to throw before poor men—some like myself with hungry babies to feed! Three hundred pounds a year! The country—the crisp, bracing air—health—strength!

MRS. JERMYN.

Delightful! That's it! That's it!

NOEL BRICE.

Three hundred pounds a year! No more anxiety! Bertha with rosy checks, and little Teddy and Blanche and the baby——

MRS. JERMYN.

Rolling upon the grass at Shodly, filling the diamond casements of the farm-house with their fresh,

ruddy faces, or making its old rooms ring with the
rattle of their metal spoons!   Oh, Mr. Brice !

NOEL BRICE.

Why, Miss Moxon, you make quite a pretty picture of it.

MRS. JERMYN.

I—oh, yes—I—can imagine little children at a
place like—what's its name ?

NOEL BRICE.

Imagine — yes.   [*Throwing the paper from him.*]
Ah, but it is wrong even to imagine it.

MRS. JERMYN.

Then you won't—try—to get there !

NOEL BRICE.

I ! My dear Miss Moxon, the air here may be thick,
murky, unwholesome, but even for fresh air and £300
a year one doesn't sell one's convictions to this in-
fatuated worshipper of the race-course.
                    [*He begins loading his pipe.*]

MRS. JERMYN.

[*To herself.*]   Poor fellow ! To see him turning
his back upon money and comfort for the sake of
his conscience—oh, it's pitiful !

NOEL BRICE.

[*Lighting his pipe.*]   I suppose that Founder, as
he calls himself, is a little mad.

MRS. JERMYN.

I really don't see any evidence of it, Mr. Brice. [*Picking up the paper and smoothing it out.*] And I must say that I am surprised, *surprised,* at your bigoted prejudice against horse-racing.

NOEL BRICE.

Prejudice, Miss Moxon !

MRS. JERMYN.

Surely anything tending to develop the wonderful capacities of a noble and intelligent animal like the horse——

NOEL BRICE.

Oh, yes, I admit that's very interesting.

MRS. JERMYN.

Certainly, and useful ; and therefore racing is and ought to be the characteristic sport of all English-men, including the clergy.

NOEL BRICE.

What is called Sport, Miss Moxon, is too often mere brutality.

MRS. JERMYN.

Brutality ! Was Adam brutal ?

NOEL BRICE.

Adam ! What Adam ?

MRS. JERMYN.

The Adam. Were there not horses in Eden ?

NOEL BRICE.

We're taught to believe so.

MRS. JERMYN.

Then, ·there, Mr. Brice, you have the origin of Ascot. The presence of Eve—no, no, she wasn't there.

NOEL BRICE.

Ha, ha! You positively overwhelm me with the weight of your theology.

MRS. JERMYN.

Ah, then, won't you write to the solicitor at New-market? For the sake of the babies — the babies——

NOEL BRICE.

My dear Miss Moxon, the babies would grow up bandy and crooked if I professed opinions I do not hold.

MRS. JERMYN.

- [*To herself.*] How is it possible to do good to such an obstinate man! Mr. Brice—Mr. Brice.

NOEL BRICE.

You're not going to crush me with Adam again, are you?

MRS. JERMYN.

No. But won't you dictate to me *some sort* of response to send to this solicitor—to please me, who am so fond of Bertha?

NOEL BRICE.

Of course I will—if you'll allow me to write quite candidly.

MRS. JERMYN.

Ah, thank you! [*Sitting at the table and addressing an envelope as she speaks to herself.*] If he would write a half-and-half sort of letter, it might do. And then, if he were appointed Warden of Shodly, and came to find out who Miss Moxon really was, he would forgive me all my deception, and perhaps learn to remember me as an angel in disguise. An angel in disguise! I have begun by disguising my hand. Mr. Pinching would never recognise that. ·[*To* NOEL.] I've addressed the envelope very neatly, Mr. Brice. Will *you* begin now?

NOEL BRICE.

H'm. [*Dictating, his back turned toward her.*] "Sir!"

MRS. JERMYN.

Dear Sir! *Dear* Sir!

NOEL BRICE.

"Sir!"

MRS. JERMYN.

[*Writing.*] Oh!

NOEL BRICE.

"I have absolutely no sympathy with any sport or pastime which has gambling and other evil passions for its accompaniment."

MRS. JERMYN.

[*To herself, without writing.*] Oh, that won't do!

Noel Brice.

"Nor do I perceive any feature in horse-racing tending to the elevation or ennoblement of the mind of man."

Mrs. Jermyn.

[*To herself.*] Oh, dear! Oh, dear! What an obstinate man!

Noel Brice.

"Of the mind of man." Have you got that?

Mrs. Jermyn.

Y-yes, Mr. Brice.

Noel Brice.

"But if you want a guardian for your people who will strive honestly to instruct, to guide, and to comfort them, I will accept your Wardenship. Your obedient servant." Blank. How does that read?

Mrs. Jermyn.

C-c-capital—the very thing. [*To herself.*] How is it possible to be philanthropic with a man like this? I can see his babies all getting weak and bony, and—— Why should I not indite *my own* sort of letter—a careful half-and-half sort of letter—and get Bertha to coax him into signing it in the morn- ing? I'll try it—it's a forlorn hope. [*Looking toward* Noel, *who has put his head back and is dozing, she begins writing.*] "My *Dear* Sir: I have read your advertisement in *The Seraphim*"—that's true; I must be strictly truthful—[*Writing.*] "and I shall be *delighted*"—[*Looking cautiously toward* Noel, *who makes no sign.*] "delighted to accept the Wardenship of your *much-needed* Home " — [*Looking up frightened.*] That's *rather* truthful. [*Writing.*] "your much needed Home for—for Disabled Horsemen." The poor fellow will like that better than Decayed Jockeys. [*Writing.*] "It would be my endeavour to reconcile my views to yours "— that's just the same thing as reconciling Spencer's views to his, of course—"and to discharge my duties according to the dictates of my conscience." Why, it's his own letter—put a little more pleasantly. [*Writing.*] " *Believe* me, my *dear* sir, *very* sincerely yours,"—space for signature. Oh, I wonder if he'll ever see it in the proper light ! Oh !

NOEL BRICE.

[*Rousing himself.*] I beg your pardon—I was half asleep.

MRS. JERMYN.

[*Holding the letter behind her.*] W-were you ?

NOEL BRICE.

Well, am I to sign the letter ?

MRS. JERMYN.

The l-l-letter !

NOEL BRICE.

About the Wardenship.

MRS. JERMYN.

Oh, that letter ! [*Producing it awkwardly.*] If you are alluding to *that* letter—I—I have that letter here.

F

NOEL BRICE.

[*Taking the letter from her, and sitting at the table, he selects a pen.*] Thank you. [*Half to himself.*] I'll just glance through it.

MRS. JERMYN.

. Oh! Mr. Brice. [*Taking the letter from him and laying it before him while she conceals the written part with her hand.*] That's where you sign—there at the bottom of the page.

NOEL BRICE.

Yes, but I was going to read it first.

MRS. JERMYN.

No, no—afterwards. Then you'll see how it looks all together, with the signature.

NOEL BRICE.

I thought perhaps it was rather too abrupt.

MRS. JERMYN.

No—it doesn't seem so very abrupt.
[*He tries to sign his name, but she nervously moves her hands over the letter to prevent his seeing its contents.*]

NOEL BRICE.

I beg your pardon—I can't write if you do that.

MRS. JERMYN.

I—I'm trying to help you.

NOEL BRICE.

[*Signing his name.*] That's it. Now, I'll——

MRS. JERMYN.

Oh, no, let me—let me read it. It's written in such an odd way. Are you ready?

NOEL BRICE.

Quite.

MRS. JERMYN.

Er—um—you're not paying attention, Mr. Brice.

NOEL BRICE.

Indeed I am.

MRS. JERMYN.

"My—dear——"

NOEL BRICE.

Eh?

MRS. JERMYN.

"Sir!"

NOEL BRICE.

Oh!

MRS. JERMYN.

"I—I——"

[TOM *and* BERTHA *suddenly enter.*]

BERTHA.

Uncle Noel!

TOM CLARK.

Look out, old fellow!

NOEL BRICE.

What's the matter?

BERTHA.

She's coming!

NOEL BRICE.

She—who?

BERTHA.

Mrs. Porcher.

NOEL BRICE.

Hush! Don't be frightened! Bring her in, Tom. [TOM *hurries out.*] Good gracious! what mischief is this old lady bent on now!

MRS. JERMYN.

[*To herself.*] Oh!—the letter! [*Folding and closing the letter.*] Ready for the post! Oh! oh! I wonder if I have done quite right?

[TOM *introduces* MRS. PORCHER, *a grim old woman in black and a formidable bonnet, who enters with a solemn glare.*]

NOEL BRICE.

Come in, Mrs. Porcher.

MRS. PORCHER.

[*Eyeing* MRS. JERMYN *severely.*] Is this the Miss Markham I hear of—the lady now in residence here?

NOEL BRICE.

This is Miss Moxon, the lady who is kind enough to be a companion to my niece. [MRS. JERMYN *bows slightly*, MRS. PORCHER *coughs asthmatically.*] Sit down, Mrs. Porcher.

[MRS. PORCHER *silently enthrones herself.*]

MRS. PORCHER.

A footstool. [BERTHA *and* TOM *fetch footstool,
which* NOEL *places· at* MRS. PORCHER's *feet.*] This is
not the complimentary hour for calling, nor is this,
I regret to say, in any sense a complimentary visit.

[BERTHA *and* TOM *retire on tiptoe into the further
room and close the folding-doors softly.*]

NOEL BRICE.

I hope at least, Mrs. Porcher——

MRS. PORCHER.

Please. But for the performance of an unpleas-
ant duty any hour seems to me appropriate.

MRS. JERMYN.

Pray allow me to leave you.

MRS. PORCHER.

Er—no. I think it would be better if Miss—Miss
Moxon would pay me the compliment of remaining.
I grieve—I grieve to say that Miss Moxon is un-
pleasantly associated with the object of my visit.

NOEL BRICE.

In which case I should prefer receiving a written
communication from you, Mrs. Porcher.

MRS. PORCHER.

I think not. The cold formula of a letter is
necessarily frigid and repellent ; in dealing a blow
the sympathetic cadences of the human voice are
much preferable. Mr. Brice, Dr. Porcher has during the term of your curacy permitted you to dis-

charge many, if not all, his duties in addition to your own. You cannot deny it.

NOEL BRICE.

It is certainly the case.

MRS. PORCHER.

I thank you for the frankness of that admission. And why is this so ? For eighteen years Dr. Porcher has not slept uninterruptedly through one entire night. My cough, commencing regularly at sundown, has not permitted him to do so. That cough being now chronic I can hope for no amelioration in the condition of Dr. Porcher. In the meantime, Mr. Brice, he is dependent on the faith, the enthusiasm, the integrity of his curate.

NOEL BRICE.

And that faith, that enthusiasm, and that integrity he has always had from me. Do you call it into question ?

MRS. PORCHER.

Pardon me? Up to about ten days ago—I think that is the time when Miss Moxon was first received into your house ?—up to that time, I—man and wife being one, I speak as Dr. Porcher—I had but slight cause for complaint.

NOEL BRICE.

Whether you speak for Dr. Porcher, or for yourself alone, or for both of you, I beg you to speak carefully.

Mrs. Porcher.

I am not, Mr. Brice, at all in the habit of trusting to inspiration. I have here memoranda. [*Referring to her tablets.*] When six weeks ago you suggested taking a short holiday, you advertised for a temporary companion for your niece—*for your niece!* Well, then, Mr. Brice, in due course this lady arrives here, and immediately relieves you of some of your duties of visiting—a thing which I, her senior if I mistake not, would hardly have presumed to do.

Noel Brice.

Well, madam, what then?

Mrs. Porcher.

Then, Mr. Brice, one would conjecture that the time had arrived for *you* to leave London.

Noel Brice.

My arrangements became altered. I had—reasons.

Mrs. Porcher.

Quite so. I feared this—I have feared this tremblingly.

Mrs. Jermyn.

You have feared what, madam?

Mrs. Porcher.

I beg your pardon?

Mrs. Jermyn.

· You have associated my name with the object of your visit here. I want to know what your fear is in connection with the abandonment of Mr. Brice's holiday.

MRS. PORCHER.

H'm! Certainly. I fear that Dr. Porcher will never be able to quite satisfy those ladies of our parish who are so concerned about this business, that Mr. Brice did not relinquish his holiday because——

MRS. JERMYN.

Because?

NOEL BRICE.

[*To* MRS. JERMYN.] Hush! [*To* MRS. PORCHER.] Please!

MRS. JERMYN.

Because?

MRS. PORCHER.

Because Mr. Brice had found not only a companion for his niece, but a companion for——

NOEL BRICE.

[*To* MRS. PORCHER, *pointing to the door.*] Leave this room!

MRS. PORCHER.

What!

NOEL BRICE.

Leave this room—my house—leave it! When can I see Dr. Porcher? It must be soon—immediately.

MRS. PORCHER.

I speak with the voice of Dr. Porcher——

NOEL BRICE.

Ah, don't you understand what I mean? That I desire to wash my hands of you all without a moment's delay! Let me be rid of you! Your money has mildewed the bread with which I feed the dear ones who are dependent upon me, long enough! Let me be rid of you!

MRS. PORCHER.

[*Producing a letter.*] Anticipating some unseemly outburst of this nature, Mr. Brice, I am armed with a letter from Dr. Porcher—written reluctantly at my dictation—informing you that Mr. Charlesworth, your dear amiable predecessor, is ready to take your place at once.

NOEL BRICE.

[*Taking the letter.*] To-morrow. Go, please. Go! [*He opens the folding-doors and calls* TOM.]

MRS. PORCHER.

[*To* MRS. JERMYN, *who is standing as if stricken, with her head drooping.*] Pardon me. The christian name, Constance, I think? [MRS. JERMYN *looks at* MRS. PORCHER *without replying.*] Constance—I remember. I shall feel it my duty to report the name of Constance Moxon, unfavourably, to the Governesses Institute.

[TOM *opens the door,* MRS. PORCHER *sails out, and he follows her.*]

NOEL BRICE.

Oh, Miss Moxon!

MRS. JERMYN.

Hush! Don't speak to me, please, Mr. Brice! Don't, don't speak to me!

[*She puts her handkerchief to her eyes;* BERTHA *runs to her side.*]

BERTHA.

What is the matter, dear? Uncle Noel, has Mrs. Porcher made Miss Moxon cry?

NOEL BRICE.

[*To* Mrs. JERMYN.] Only say that you can pardon me for never suspecting that this woman's—that any woman's — malice could go to such a monstrous length!

Mrs. JERMYN.

[*Softly to* NOEL.] Hush!—Bertha. Mrs. Porcher is very angry, Bertha, because your uncle has not taken his holiday—so terribly angry. Mr. Brice, pray don't give another thought to my share in the matter — never let it cross your mind again. Oh, how dare she! how dare she!

BERTHA.

But why are you crying so, dear?

Mrs. JERMYN.

I—oh, I am crying a little, Bertha—because I have to run away from you very suddenly. I leave this house to-night--at once. [NOEL *starts.*]

BERTHA.

To-night! Not for good!

Mrs. JERMYN.

Yes—for good. I am of no use, you know—because—because your uncle has not gone for his holiday.

BERTHA.

Oh, why don't you persuade her to stay, Uncle Noel?

MRS. JERMYN.

Hush, dear! Come with me.

NOEL BRICE.

Miss Moxon!

MRS. JERMYN.

[*Turning to* NOEL.] Don't—please—please! Oh, Mr. Brice, why, why couldn't you have gone for your holiday! [*She goes out with* BERTHA.]

NOEL BRICE.

Oh, the insult to her—and under my roof! The insult to her! The insult to her whose smile does more to brighten this parish than all the sun that ever finds its way here! [*Crushing* PORCHER's *letter in his hand.*] My formal dismissal from Dr. Porcher. He shall see me to-morrow. I need not curb my tongue to him in defence of the woman I love—oh, at least I can speak the words to myself—the woman I love!

[TOM *enters.*]

TOM CLARK.

What has the old lady done now, Noel?

NOEL BRICE.

I'm out of St. Jacob's, Tom.

TOM CLARK.

Are you, Noel? Then so am I. Mind, you don't

shake me off—I'm after you and Bertha, wherever you go.

NOEL BRICE.

But I haven't told you the worst of it, my boy.

TOM CLARK.

Why, what's wrong?

NOEL BRICE.

She has robbed me of—of a friend—a friend I can't spare. Her bitter tongue is driving Miss Moxon away from us to-night, and—and—ah, Tom, you're little more than a boy, and don't understand, and I can't tell you!

TOM CLARK.

Little more than a boy, am I! Can't understand, can't I! Why, Noel, I'm in love too!

NOEL BRICE.

What do you mean by you're in love *too?*

TOM CLARK.

I mean I love Bertha!

NOEL BRICE.

Tom Clark!

TOM CLARK.

Why, what a fool I should be if I didn't! Ah, Noel, love gives a fellow a pair of spectacles, which enables him to see right through another fellow's waistcoat and straight into his heart. Ha, ha! Why, old chap, I guessed it a week ago!

NOEL BRICE.

I don't know what you mean! A week ago! Why, Tom, *I* didn't know it then!

TOM CLARK.

No, but the man himself is always the last to find it out. Oh, I'm so glad, old chap!

NOEL BRICE.

Glad!

TOM CLARK.

You know I shouldn't have liked you to marry anybody I didn't quite approve of. But I do admire her—so does Bertha. I think we're both to be congratulated, eh?

NOEL BRICE.

Be quiet! Don't go on in that way, Tom—I can't bear it! She's leaving me—I may never see her again. And even if these few past happy days could go on unbrokenly for years to come, I could never open my lips about love. Why, man, how could I?

TOM CLARK.

How could you! Oh, I'll tell you *how*.

NOEL BRICE.

Will you be quiet, Tom! You know I haven't a penny in the world.

TOM CLARK.

Well, no more have I—and I proposed half an hour ago.

[BERTHA *enters*.]

BERTHA.

[*Crying.*] Tom, will you g-g-go and find a c-c-cab to take Miss Moxon away?

TOM CLARK.

[*Whispering.*] Bertha, dear, let us look for it together. I think Noel has something awfully important to tell Miss Moxon. Hush! [*Looking at* NOEL.] Dear old Noel! I think he's a lucky chap after all.

[TOM *and* BERTHA *go quietly out. The room is growing gradually darker.* MRS. JERMYN *enters.*]

MRS. JERMYN.

[*Looking about her.*] Bertha! Bertha! [*She sees* NOEL. *To herself.*] Where is Bertha? Poor fellow—I didn't want to say good-bye to him alone.

NOEL BRICE.

[*Facing her suddenly.*] You are going away, then —really going away?

MRS. JERMYN.

Yes. I—I am waiting for a cab, Mr. Brice.

NOEL BRICE.

The thought that you are driven away from us in such an infamous manner is maddening to me.

MRS. JERMYN.

Oh, you mustn't let other people's ill-nature hurt you so much. As for myself, I was going to-morrow —a few hours earlier, what can it matter?

NOEL BRICE.

No, no, that's true ! What can it matter? But I —Bertha and I—were rather dull and lonely here when you found us, and somehow you—as a new-comer often will——

MRS. JERMYN.

Oh, yes—a strange face does break the monotony of life, doesn't it ?

NOEL BRICE.

Yes. And when one loses that face, when it has ceased to be a strange one ; when one enters a room thinking to see a familiar form in that corner or in that, and is almost startled to find — nothing — then——

MRS. JERMYN.

Then one is pained, naturally—for a day or two.

NOEL BRICE.

Yes, I mean—for a day or two.
[*He turns away from her and goes to the window.*]

MRS. JERMYN.

Is that a cab at our door ?

NOEL BRICE.

Yes.　　　[*He goes to the door and opens it.*]

MRS. JERMYN.

[*To herself.*]　I am glad the time has come.

NOEL BRICE.

[*To himself.*] Some people asking for Tom. They have gone upstairs to his room.

[*He closes the door.*]

MRS. JERMYN.

Good-bye, then, Mr. Brice.

NOEL BRICE.

[*Taking her hand.*] Good-bye. Miss Moxon, will you, as the parting act of a friend, solve a problem which arises in the life of every poor man and which to-night crosses me in mine? You know how poor I am—how prospectless, saddled with cares, almost without worldly hope. But I have never despaired till to-night—and yet till to-night I have not been so near setting foot upon a path full of encouragement and light. I am at the cross-roads of life—read for me the index which points this way or that!

MRS. JERMYN.

Of course I will help you if I can, Mr. Brice. What is your trouble?

[*The room is now almost in darkness.*]

NOEL BRICE.

There is a woman I love—whom I love as I love no other earthly being. Tell me—could I approach her with such a tale of poverty and struggle upon my lips as I have told you, my friend? What would she say to me if I presumed to ask her to be my wife?

Mrs. Jermyn.

Surely, if she loved you, she would trudge the hard road with you.

Noel Brice.

But is it not woman-like to fear poverty?

Mrs. Jermyn.

Yes, to fear and to face it.

Noel Brice.

You bid me speak to her then?

Mrs. Jermyn.

If you trust her, yes.

Noel Brice.

Then give me your hand again.

Mrs. Jermyn.

Mr. Brice!

Noel Brice.

[*Taking her hand.*] And let me speak to you!

Mrs. Jermyn.

To me?

Noel Brice.

To you—the woman I love with all my heart.

Mrs. Jermyn.

[*Retreating from him slowly, as if in a dream.*] The woman *you* love! [*Under her breath.*] Oh, what have I done?

[Jermyn *appears at the door, but neither* Noel *nor* Mrs. Jermyn *hears or sees him.*]

G

NOEL BRICE.

Speak to me, friend! Still friend—the dearest name a man can give even the woman he would make his wife!

[NOEL *seizes her hand.* JERMYN *retreats and closes the door sharply.*]

MRS. JERMYN.

Hush! Oh, hush!

NOEL BRICE.

Who's there? Who's there?

[JERMYN *knocks, then reopens the door and enters.* MRS. JERMYN *crouches behind the arm-chair.*]

SPENCER JERMYN.

I really must apologize. I'm afraid you didn't hear me knock.

NOEL BRICE.

Have you any business with me? My name is Brice.

SPENCER JERMYN.

My dear sir, I'm pleased to meet you. I'm told you're a great friend of my son.

NOEL BRICE.

Your son?

SPENCER JERMYN.

My son, Allan Jermyn—the boy who calls himself Tom Clark.

NOEL BRICE.

Allan Jermyn—Tom Clark !

[*With a stifled cry* MRS. JERMYN, *hiding her face, staggers into the further room and shuts the folding-doors, at the same moment* PINCHING *appears in the doorway.*]

PINCHING.

Jermyn ! Here's the boy ! Allan ! [ALLAN *enters with* BERTHA.] Allan !

ALLAN.

[*Grasping* PINCHING'S *hand boisterously.*] Ralph ! Good gracious me ! Well, I never ! How did you find me out ? Never mind. How's my father ? Does he ever ask about me ? Well, I am glad to see you ! Here, Noel ! Noel ! [BERTHA *lights the gas.*]

PINCHING.

[*Pointing to* JERMYN.] Look there.

ALLAN.

Father !

SPENCER JERMYN.

Allan, my boy !

[*They are about to embrace effusively, when they simultaneously draw back and look at each other.*]

ALLAN.

Hallo, father ! How are you ?

SPENCER JERMYN.

H'm ! Do you know you were very disrespectful to me when I last had the pleasure of seeing you, sir ?

ALLAN.

I'm sorry you think so, father.

SPENCER JERMYN.

I do more than think so, sir—I'm sure of it.

PINCHING.

Jermyn, Jermyn—Allan, my boy!

SPENCER JERMYN.

Well, I don't know—however — [*taking* ALLAN's *hand*] I'm pretty well, thank ye.

ALLAN.

Glad to see you, dad.   Backed any of the wrong 'uns lately?

SPENCER JERMYN.

What do you mean by that?   Don't you dare to mention King Caraway——

PINCHING.

Allan—Jermyn—no, no!

ALLAN.

Beg pardon, father. Noel!   [*To* JERMYN.]   This is Mr. Brice—the Rev. Noel Brice—the dearest fellow in the world—my true friend.

[JERMYN *shakes hands with* NOEL.]

NOEL BRICE.

Ah, Tom, Tom, I was Tom Clark's friend; but I'm quite a stranger to Allan Jermyn.

ALLAN.

I was going to spin you the whole yarn to-night; wasn't I, Bertha?

SPENCER JERMYN.

Eh?

ALLAN.

Oh—Bertha. Mr. Brice's niece, Bertha—the dearest fellow in the world—I mean, another friend of mine.   [JERMYN *bows.*]

BERTHA.

[*Quietly to* ALLAN.]   Oh, Allan, I'm so afraid.

ALLAN.

Afraid, my darling?

BERTHA.

In the hat-shop you were all mine. Now I feel towards you as I do towards the books from the lending library. The chapters of your life are not for me alone, and when you leave me other people may take you in and turn you up at the corners.

ALLAN.

No, never this book, Bertha.

BERTHA.

Oh, Allan, Allan, you'll always be Tom to me, won't you, dear?

[*The folding-doors slightly open and* MRS. JERMYN
   *looks eagerly at the outer door for means of es-
   cape, but draws back quickly.*]

SPENCER JERMYN.

[*To* NOEL.] A brave young fellow, you think him, do you? You're right, sir. Mr. Brice, let me call you a friend of mine. Allan!

ALLAN.

[*Turning from* BERTHA.] Yes, father.

SPENCER JERMYN.

You'll return with me to the hotel to-night.

BERTHA.

Oh!

SPENCER JERMYN.

To-morrow we'll pop down to Ascot to see the running for the Gold Cup—next day I shall take you home. Do you know that your mother is dying with curiosity to see what her son is like?

ALLAN.

I shall be happy to make her acquaintance, father.

SPENCER JERMYN.

Good-night, Mr. Brice.

[MRS. JERMYN *again attempts to make her escape.*]

PINCHING.

[*Holding a note he has just scribbled.*] May I ask you, Mr. Brice, to give this note to Inspector Mason when he calls to-night? It is to let him know the result of our search for Allan. I'll place it here. [*Laying it carelessly on the writing-table and seeing the letter addressed to himself.*] Dear me! Pardon me.

I think this is addressed to me—Pinching, of New-market.

[MRS. JERMYN *staggers back into the further room.*]

NOEL BRICE.

I certainly have written a letter to a Mr. Pinching, Solicitor, of Newmarket.

PINCHING.

[*Pointing to the newspaper.*] In reference to an advertisement in *The Seraphim*, may I ask?

NOEL BRICE.

Yes.

SPENCER JERMYN.

Not applying for the Wardenship of the Home at Shodly Heath?

NOEL BRICE.

Well—yes.

PINCHING.

[*Opening the letter.*] Will you allow me? I am the Mr. Pinching.

NOEL BRICE.

Certainly.

SPENCER JERMYN.

Good gracious me, Mr. Brice! And I, sir, *I* am the Founder!

ALLAN.

Why, Noel, what's all this about?

PINCHING.

Jermyn!

[JERMYN *reads the letter with* PINCHING, *excitedly.*]

SPENCER JERMYN.

Dear me, this is quite extraordinary! Excuse me. [*Taking the letter.*] My dear Pinching! We have found the young liberal-minded sporting parson! Diana said there wasn't one in existence!

ALLAN.

Oh, Noel, here's a stroke of luck!

BERTHA.

Oh, Uncle Noel!

SPENCER JERMYN.

Pinching! the first, the only answer to our advertisement—the very man! [*To* NOEL, *enthusiastically.*] Mr. Brice, there is no time to lose in a scheme like this. When can you come down to Shodly?

ALLAN.

Directly, dad. Old Noel at Shodly! Bertha! Five miles from Odlum House! Dad, you've got hold of the finest chap in the world!

NOEL BRICE.

But, Mr. Jermyn, do you really mean that you can accept the propositions contained in that letter?

SPENCER JERMYN.

Never read a letter that pleased me better in my life! Pinching, will you take Mr. Brice down to the Home by the eleven-fifty-five to-morrow morning?

PINCHING.

By all means, if he agrees.

[MRS. JERMYN, *with a horror-stricken face, comes from the folding-doors and creeps gradually towards the door.*]

SPENCER JERMYN.

Mr. Brice, my son's friends are mine—things happen strangely. [*Taking* NOEL'S *hand.*] Let me express a hope that you may long remain Warden of Shodly. Come along, Allan !

ALLAN.

[*Waving his hat.*] The Warden of Shodly ! Hurrah !

[MRS. JERMYN, *unperceived, staggers out at the door.*]

END OF THE SECOND ACT.

THE THIRD ACT.

The scene is an elegant morning-room at MR. JER-
MYN'S, *with French windows, a veranda, and a
conservatory, and a view of the garden beyond.
It is morning, and the breakfast things are on a
table placed at the entrance to the conservatory.*
MISS MOXON *is sitting alone at the breakfast-
table.*

MISS MOXON.

Here's Ralph ! [*Going to the window and waving
her handkerchief.*] Oh, what a depressed object he
looks !

[PINCHING *enters, looking very miserable, with a telegram in his hand.*]

PINCHING.

Oh, good-morning, Constance.

MISS MOXON.

Good-morning !

PINCHING.

How are you this morning ?

Miss Moxon.

Beyond wishing I were dead I'm extremely well, thank you. [*He kisses her upon the forehead abstractedly.*] On the brow.

Pinching.

Where's Mrs. Jermyn?

Miss Moxon.

Pacing up and down the hall distractedly. There's her breakfast untouched. I've had mine.

Pinching.

We're stuck knee-deep in a nice substantial quagmire, I must say. [*Showing the telegram.*] Mr. Jermyn and Allan have left London this morning by the early train, and will be home in about twenty minutes. The Prodigal's Return.

[Miss Moxon *gently falls against* Pinching, *holding on to his arm.*]

Miss Moxon.

Oh, Ralph—Ralph!

Pinching.

[*Studying the telegram intently.*] Not just now, Constance, dear—not just now, my love.

Miss Moxon.

I must—for I am so sorry for you.

Pinching.

Sorry for *me?* Why on *my* account particularly?

Miss Moxon.

Of course I am sorry too for poor Diana and for Mr. Jermyn, and for that innocent clergyman at Shodly—their troubles are to come——

Pinching.

You are sorry for yourself also, Constance, I hope —you originated the whole mischief, if you remember.

Miss Moxon.

I know I did ; but then, being engaged, the gentleman takes the entire responsibility. [*Leaning her head on his shoulder.*] And that must be so awful where the gentleman's a solicitor.

Pinching.

You are right, Constance—it is awful, shockingly awful. Oh, Constance, my dear girl, if less than a fortnight ago you had but confided to me the whereabouts of Mrs. Jermyn I could have flown up to London, dragged her back by a few sensible words of advice, and saved everybody the catastrophe which is to break over our heads this morning like the culminating outburst of a grand pyrotechnic display. Oh ! oh ! oh !

Miss Moxon.

It was Diana's secret—do you blame me for keeping it ?

Pinching.

Look at the result !

Miss Moxon.

I am the first woman who has ever kept a secret

for a whole fortnight. You ought to worship me
for it!

PINCHING.

I do—I do. But never do such a thing again,
Constance!

MISS MOXON.

Besides, why blame *me?* Who was it who led
Mr. Jermyn, the night before last, into the very
house in which his wife was? You're a lawyer—
where was your instinct?

PINCHING.

A lawyer doesn't run along with his nose on the
ground like a pointer!

MISS MOXON.

I don't know what a lawyer does, I'm sure. All
my theories about lawyers are crumbling—my illu-
sions used to be beautiful. I begin to be sorry I
ever met a solicitor.

PINCHING.

Constance, my dear, solicitors are but men!

MISS MOXON.

Under the peculiar circumstances it isn't for me to
object to that; but your bringing this Mr. Brice
down to Shodly yesterday and installing him within
five miles of the very rug we're standing on! How
could you? How could you? How could you?

PINCHING.

How was I to know that the poor man was madly
in love with Diana Jermyn, *alias* Constance Moxon?

Miss Moxon.

Don't argue intemperately, *please*. There is about a quarter of an hour to decide—what is to be done?

Pinching.

Oh, the case is clear enough—h'm !

Miss Moxon.

H'm ! Now then.

Pinching.

First gently acquaint Mr. Brice that he has formed an attachment to Tom Clark's — that is, Allan Jermyn's—father's wife, who is Miss Moxon.

Miss Moxon.

No, no—first let Allan Jermyn know that his father's wife is his mother.

Pinching.

Whose mother, my dear?

Miss Moxon.

Don't interrupt me. Tell Allan Jermyn that he is Constance Moxon's son.

Pinching.

No, no, I don't like the idea of that—it doesn't put me in a nice position. The case is quite simple. First tell Jermyn that Mr. Brice is in love with Mrs. Jermyn. That's easy enough.

Miss Moxon.

Oh, yes, that's all right. And who's going to transact that nice little easy bit of business?

PINCHING.

Who!

MISS MOXON.

It sounds like the solicitor's department.

PINCHING.

No, no—it is purely a woman's task.

MISS MOXON.

Diana's?

PINCHING.

My dear girl, can we expect a wife to tell her husband that another man has proposed to her? Put yourself in that position—no, don't do that—I mean—— The whole thing's in a nutshell. You've known Mrs. Jermyn since childhood.

MISS MOXON.

I do it! Oh, Ralph, what an unmanly proposal!

PINCHING.

Who *is* to do it then?

MISS MOXON.

Would Mr. Brice like to help? He's the nearest clergyman!

PINCHING.

Help to let Jermyn know that he loves—— Oh, Constance!

MISS MOXON.

Very well, then, we are forced to return to the only disinterested person—the young family solicitor.

PINCHING.

Disinterested! When the original mischief arose from a suggestion of the lady I'm engaged to marry!

MISS MOXON.

Ralph Pinching!

PINCHING.

My dear!

MISS MOXON.

Ralph Pinching—of Newmarket! That is about the fiftieth time you have upbraided me with my innocent complicity in this unfortunate business. I ask you one question—do you wish to break it off?

PINCHING.

Of course I don't, my dear girl.

MISS MOXON.

Very well, then, I do. I literally sicken of this never-ending cruelty.

PINCHING.

Cruelty—Constance, darling!

MISS MOXON.

You can be gentle at times, but your gentleness is that of the summer sky, which anon sends forth its fiery shaft to ignite and to destroy, Mr. Pinching.

PINCHING.

My dear girl, you know you don't mean—— .

MISS MOXON.

I mean that I must be quite perfect in the eyes

of the man I marry. The chains of our engagement have clanked for a fortnight, Ralph Pinching ;
let mine be the hand to strike them from your
chafing limbs. Good-morning !
[*She goes out through the window.*]

PINCHING.

We have the same scene regularly every day, and
in very nearly the same language. [*Studying the telegram again.*] But I can't think of my own bothers
with so many of other people's to distract me. Now,
what——

[*Miss Moxon re-enters and comes to* PINCHING.]

MISS MOXON.

Ralph, dear.

PINCHING.

Ah, my darling !

MISS MOXON.

I have carefully thought over our recent interview.

PINCHING.

Which one, Constance ?

MISS MOXON.

The one we had just now—and I have come to the
conclusion that we ought to be much more mutually
tolerant. All these sad misunderstandings are the
common incidents of long engagements.

PINCHING.

[*Intent on the telegram.*] Yes, dear, yes—they are
—they are !

H

Miss Moxon.

You will forget what I said to you, won't you?

Pinching.

I do forget it, my darling—entirely.

Miss Moxon.

Forget—and forgive?

Pinching.

Certainly. [*He kisses her forehead in an absent way.*]

Miss Moxon.

[*To herself.*] On the brow.

Pinching.

[*Looking toward the conservatory.*] Mrs. Jermyn!

[Mrs. Jermyn *enters through the conservatory. She is pale, her eyes are fixed upon the ground, her arms hang listlessly down, she holds a telegram.*]

Miss Moxon.

Di, dear.

Mrs. Jermyn.

Constance.

[*She puts her lips to* Miss Moxon's *forehead, then sinks upon the settee.*]

Miss Moxon.

[*To herself.*] On the brow. You look very white, Diana.

Mrs. Jermyn.

I feel white.

Miss Moxon.

You didn't sleep again last night?

Mrs. Jermyn.

Do I look as if I had slept?

Miss Moxon.

Two nights without rest—hot hands—a galloping pulse. Oh, Diana, can't you—can't you eat an egg?

Mrs. Jermyn.

Oh, please.

Miss Moxon.

I've had an egg, and do I look as if *I'd* slept?

Mrs. Jermyn.

Yes, Connie, dear, you do.

Miss Moxon.

Well, that's not my fault! Why don't you all say you blame me for what has happened! Oh, why was I born!

Mrs. Jermyn.

[*Her eyes fixed upon the telegram.*] Oh, don't go back to years ago, Connie!

Miss Moxon.

Diana!

Mrs. Jermyn.

I mean the present is so terribly exigent.

Miss Moxon.

Before Mr. Pinching, too!

Mrs. Jermyn.

Mr. Pinching!

MISS MOXON.

He's here. [*To* PINCHING, *whom she brings forward.*] Poor Di wanders a little—she imagines that some things happened long ago.

MRS. JERMYN.

[*Shaking hands feebly with* PINCHING.] Good-morning.

PINCHING.

I see you have received a telegram.

MRS. JERMYN.

Yes—from my husband. [*Reading.*] "Burlington—Cork Street. The boy most anxious to be presented to his mother—thinks you're a dowager—haven't undeceived him. Peppercorn picked up the Gold Cup. Expect us, without fail, by evening train."

PINCHING.

[*Looking at* MRS. JERMYN's *telegram.*] Excuse me—thank you. [*To* MISS MOXON.] There's a discrepancy between our telegrams—they've written "evening" train in Mrs. Jermyn's, and "early" train in mine.

MISS MOXON.

Then she doesn't know they may be here in ten minutes.

PINCHING.

No—you'd better tell her.

Miss Moxon.

No—*you'd* better tell her.

Pinching.

Yes—but I thought as you're a woman— —

Miss Moxon.

I know—but you being a solicitor——

Pinching.

Yes, I know, but——   [*They argue.*]

Mrs. Jermyn.

Mr. Pinching.

Pinching.

Mrs. Jermyn.

Mrs. Jermyn.

I believe you have been made acquainted with all the details of this dreadful business.

Pinching.

Constance has told me everything.

Mrs. Jermyn.

At my request. You—you are a solicitor.

Miss Moxon.

That's what *I* say!

Mrs. Jermyn.

At an hour like this one naturally gets a crumb of comfort from the clear brain and calm judgment of a man like yourself.

PINCHING.

You're very good—I—anything I can do——

MRS. JERMYN.

Thank you. I think you had better tell me about this clergyman—Mr. Brice. I understand you brought him from London to Shodly yesterday morning?

PINCHING.

With his niece—yes.

MRS. JERMYN.

Did he make any reference to—to—you know whom I mean—to me?

PINCHING.

He did. When I called for him in the morning I found him in great distress of mind. At first he declined to accompany me. I asked him why. He replied that he had sustained a great loss—a most precious friend had gone from him. I asked in what way. He said as if the earth had swallowed her. "A lady, then?" I said. "Yes," he replied, "the brightest, the sweetest, the dearest lady in the world."

MRS. JERMYN.

Thank you, Mr. Pinching. I would rather hear no more.

MISS MOXON.

[*To* PINCHING, *shaking her head.*] Be quiet, be quiet!

Mrs. Jermyn.

[*To* Pinching, *commanding herself.*] But he *did* travel with you to Shodly after all?

Pinching.

At my persuasion.

Mrs. Jermyn.

Oh, yes. And you left Mr. Brice and his niece at the Farm?

Pinching.

I did!

Mrs. Jermyn.

Thank you, Mr. Pinching. I have thought everything over carefully and, I hope, conscientiously. The first thing to be done before my husband and his son return to-night——

[Pinching *and* Miss Moxon *exchange looks.*]

Pinching.

To-night——

Mrs. Jermyn.

Is to let Mr. Brice hear the whole truth. Will you start for Shodly Heath at once, Mr. Pinching? [Pinching *bows.*] Tell Mr. Brice the history of the foolish mistake—tell him that I entreat his pardon for causing him so much—so much inconvenience, and beg him to understand that I cannot do this— in person. At once, please.

Pinching.

At once.

[HEWETT *enters.*]

HEWETT.

[*Breathlessly.*] I beg your pardon, ma'am!

MRS. JERMYN.

What is it?

HEWETT.

You forgot to order the carriage, ma'am, to meet the master and Mr. Allan!

MRS. JERMYN.

Why, Hewett, they don't leave London till the evening train.

HEWETT.

Lor' bless me, I've just seen 'em drive up to the lodge in an 'ired fly!

MRS. JERMYN.

[*Clinging to* MISS MOXON.] Oh!

        [HEWETT *runs out at the window.*]

PINCHING.

I was afraid of this—my telegram said the early train.

MRS. JERMYN.

And you never told me!

MISS MOXON.

Oh, what a solicitor!

PINCHING.

I thought of mentioning it!

MRS. JERMYN.

Thought!

PINCHING.

This business quite upsets me—it's all through being engaged to one of the ladies concerned!

MRS. JERMYN.

Oh!

MISS MOXON.

Perhaps you wish to break it off, Mr. Pinching!

SPENCER JERMYN.

[*Speaking outside.*] Come through here, Allan! Hewett!

MRS. JERMYN.

Ah!

[MRS. JERMYN *drags* MISS MOXON *out at the window as* JERMYN *enters with* ALLAN.]

SPENCER JERMYN.

Ah, Pinching, here you are. Both friendly and business-like of you to be here to receive me. [*Looking at* PINCHING.] What's wrong? Aren't you well?

ALLAN.

You do look seedy, Ralph.

SPENCER JERMYN.

Tell me—you got Mr. Brice down to Shodly yesterday?

PINCHING.

Oh, yes—he's there!

SPENCER JERMYN.

That's capital—capital! So the Home's fairly
started, eh? I'm proud of what we've done, Pinching—proud, sir. It's the culminating point in my
Turf career!

[HEWETT *is passing toward the conservatory carrying*
bags and umbrellas.]

SPENCER JERMYN.

Where's your mistress, Hewett?

HEWETT.

I don't know, sir; the ladies were here a minute
ago.

SPENCER JERMYN.

The ladies! What ladies?

HEWETT.

The mistress and Miss Moxon, sir.

[*Goes through the conservatory.*]

ALLAN.

Miss Moxon?

SPENCER JERMYN.

[*To* PINCHING.] Miss Moxon is staying with us
again then?

PINCHING.

Y-yes—she's here!

SPENCER JERMYN.

She must have just returned from town?

PINCHING.

Yes—ah—just returned.

SPENCER JERMYN.

I was quite astonished when Allan casually mentioned yesterday that a Miss Moxon had been acting as companion to Mr. Brice's niece. You couldn't have known it either?

PINCHING.

No, I didn't know it!

SPENCER JERMYN.

We little thought the night before last that we were in the very house with the lady you have the happiness to—— Excuse me, Pinching—don't think me rude—one moment. [PINCHING *sits at the table.*] [*To* ALLAN.] Allan, my boy—it just strikes me. It's a very awkward thing, this attachment you've told me about, of your friend, Mr. Brice, to Miss Moxon. You know she's engaged to be married to Pinching.

ALLAN.

It *is* jolly awkward, father.

SPENCER JERMYN.

I don't like it. She's an old friend of your mother's, but I can't have a woman down here playing fast and loose with two good fellows.

ALLAN.

- Miss Moxon is a very nice woman!

SPENCER JERMYN.

Ah, they're all nice till they're found out, my boy.

I shall talk to Diana about it. Poor Pinching—I knew his father.

ALLAN.

Poor devil!

SPENCER JERMYN.

Be careful not to alarm him yet awhile. [PINCHING *is about to go out at the window.*] Wait for me here, Pinching, please.

PINCHING.

Certainly.

ALLAN.

[*Seeing the breakfast-table.*] By Jove, here's some food! I'm starving!

SPENCER JERMYN.

All right—I'll go upstairs and find your mother. Allan, my boy, I've kept it from you as long as I can, but—but—your mother isn't an old lady at all, sir!

ALLAN.

She isn't, father?

SPENCER JERMYN.

No, sir, nor a middle-aged lady—she is a young lady, much too young to own a great hulking boy like you, you young scamp, you!

ALLAN.

Ha, ha, ha!

SPENCER JERMYN.

You think I can't play a good joke, eh? Ha, ha!

[*Looking at* Pinching.] Poor Pinching—I knew his father, too!
[*He goes through the conservatory.* Allan *seats himself at the breakfast-table.*]

ALLAN.

[*Cutting a loaf.*] This comes of dad dragging me away from the breakfast-table this morning.

[Mrs. Jermyn *and* Miss Moxon *appear outside the window, and* Miss Moxon *enters on tiptoe, while* Mrs. Jermyn *shrinks back out of sight.*]

Miss Moxon.

[*Clinging to* Pinching.] Ralph—Ralph—something must be done!

Pinching.

[*In a fluster.*] I know—I know—I was just thinking of doing something.

Miss Moxon.

Look at him eating happily. [*She coughs;* Allan *rises with his mouth full.*] Mr. Jermyn's son?

Allan.

I beg your pardon. [*To himself.*] By Jove, she is a pretty woman! [*To her.*] I think I can guess who it is.

Pinching.

Oh!

Miss Moxon.

No you can't!

Allan.

Father has gone and spoilt his own joke. I hope

you don't think me too big to let me call you, for once at least, my mother.

[*He draws* Miss Moxon *to him and kisses her.*]

PINCHING.

No, no!

MISS MOXON.

[*Drawing back.*] Oh, dear! [*To herself.*] On the lips.

PINCHING.

You know that's a grown-up man, Constance—I don't care about it.

MISS MOXON.

That's right—blame *me!* Mr. Jermyn, we are all liable to error.

ALLAN.

Error! What error?

MISS MOXON.

[*Pointing to* PINCHING.] This gentleman should have spoken earlier. My name is Constance Moxon!

ALLAN.

Your name Constance Moxon!

MISS MOXON.

Indeed, yes. Diana! Diana, dear! [*Running to the window and bringing* MRS. JERMYN.] This is Mrs. Jermyn—this is your new mother.

[MRS. JERMYN *stands before* ALLAN *with her head bowed.*]

ALLAN.

[*To* Mrs. JERMYN.] Mother! Oh, Miss Moxon!
[*Looking from one to the other.*] Why——

Mrs. JERMYN.

No, that lady is right, Allan. *She* is Miss Moxon,
not I—I am Mrs. Jermyn.

MISS MOXON.

[*To* PINCHING.] No solicitor could have managed
that better.

ALLAN.

You Mrs. Jermyn!

Mrs. JERMYN.

Yes—yes.

ALLAN.

I am afraid there is some mistake. Noel—Noel
knows you are Miss Moxon.

Mrs. JERMYN.

No—he only thinks he knows I'm Miss Moxon.

ALLAN.

But father knows you were at Mr. Brice's—I told
him so.

Mrs. JERMYN.

You couldn't have done so—you didn't know I
was at Mr. Brice's.

ALLAN.

Oh, don't say that—we were there together.

Mrs. JERMYN.

But you never guessed I was your mother?

ALLAN.

No.

MRS. JERMYN.

Then how could you have told your father?

ALLAN.

I mean I told him Miss Moxon was there.

MRS. JERMYN.

Well, there is Miss Moxon.

ALLAN.

Then it seems I've told a lie to father.

MISS MOXON.

Yes, you appear to have made a very bad beginning.

ALLAN.

[*To* MRS. JERMYN.] Good gracious! Well, but—father knows that Noel's in love with you—[*to* MISS MOXON] no, it's with you!

PINCHING.

No, it isn't!

MRS. JERMYN.

Who told him that?

ALLAN.

I mentioned it.

MRS. JERMYN.

How dare you?

MISS MOXON.

Haven't you any business to mind of your own?

ALLAN.

I'm very sorry.

MRS. JERMYN.

Sorry!

ALLAN.

Father *asked* me to tell him all about it.

MRS. JERMYN.

That's impossible.

ALLAN.

He did—because he accidentally strayed into the room while Noel was proposing to you—[*to* MISS MOXON] no, I mean to *you!*

PINCHING.

No, you don't!

MRS. JERMYN.

Great Heaven! What will he think of me?

MISS MOXON.

What *does* he think of *me?*

ALLAN.

But it was in the dark.

MRS. JERMYN.

Oh!

MISS MOXON.

In the dark! That makes it worse! Oh, Diana! you never told me you didn't have the lamp lighted!

I

ALLAN.

I see how awkward it is—because one of you is engaged to Mr. Pinching.

MISS MOXON.

I am engaged to Mr. Pinching.

PINCHING.

Certainly.

ALLAN.

Of course—then it isn't nice for Pinching, is it?

PINCHING.

Yes, it is!

MISS MOXON.

Yes, it's all right for Pinching.

ALLAN.

No, it isn't — because—— No — by Jove— it's father it isn't nice for!

[MRS. JERMYN *throws herself on to the settee.*]

MRS. JERMYN.

Allan—Allan—come to me.

ALLAN.

Oh, don't cry, Miss Moxon—I mean, mother.

MRS. JERMYN.

I thought our first meeting, whenever it happened, would be so different from this.

ALLAN.

So it was, you know.

Mrs. Jermyn.

I have often pictured my husband's son as the bright impulsive young fellow you are. Have you never thought of what *I* might be?

Allan.

Well, yes, if you remember, I imagined you a thin, pale lady with spectacles——

Mrs. Jermyn.

Oh, yes, of course—that was unkind of you, Tom —I mean, Allan. But didn't your father describe me to you, dear?

Allan.

Yes, he told me yesterday you were an enormous· ly stout old lady——

Mrs. Jermyn.

Oh!

Allan.

It was his little joke, you know.

Mrs. Jermyn.

Then he hasn't told you of my fierce philanthropic cravings—my wild fancies for adopting and rearing l-l-little b-b-boys?

Allan.

No. Oh, I see——

Mrs. Jermyn.

Yes, you see, Allan, what led me into this mad scheme of taking Constance Moxon's name and filling her place at poor Mr. Brice's unknown to every· one. You don't blame your poor mother, do you?

ALLAN.

No, mother dear—of course I don't. I understand now all about it. Visiting Tyke's Court, eh?

MRS. JERMYN.

[*Crying.*] Y-yes.

ALLAN.

Ha! ha! That was rather a failure, wasn't it?

MRS. JERMYN.

[*Laughing and crying.*] Awful. Don't remind me of it!

ALLAN.

Your turning faint and coming to in the chemist's! Ha! ha!

MRS. JERMYN.

Ha! ha! Why, I should never have been so foolish if I had always had you to manage and control, my *own* dear little boy.

ALLAN.

No, mother dear.

MRS. JERMYN.

[*Smoothing his hair and arranging his cravat.*] I shall dress you quite differently from this in a day or two.

ALLAN.

Yes, mother.

MRS. JERMYN.

Yes—and I think I shall part your hair in *that* way.

ALLAN.

Thank you, mother.

Mrs. Jermyn.

And you'll always look up to me and come to me for advice in your little troubles, won't you?

Allan.

Certainly. And I should like to say, mother dear, that I am very sorry—very sorry—that I——

Mrs. Jermyn.

You are going to confess a fault, my boy?

Allan.

Well, yes, mother—I suppose I am.

Mrs. Jermyn.

Sit there. What is it, child?
[Allan *sits at her feet, she places her hand on his head.*]

Allan.

I was going to say that I——

Mrs. Jermyn.

Yes—don't be afraid that I shall punish you, Allan. You are very sorry that you——

Allan.

That I advised old Noel to—to propose to you, mother dear.

Mrs. Jermyn.

You advised him!

Allan.

Yes, mother—he wouldn't have done it but for me. I egged him on.

Mrs. Jermyn.

You did! [*Seizing him by the shoulders.*] You are the cause of all the mischief, then!

Allan.

Yes, mother, but listen!

Mrs. Jermyn.

[*Rising and facing him.*] Oh! Oh! Why aren't you the same size as other mothers' boys, that I might properly chastise you!

[Jermyn *bustles in at the window.*]

Spencer Jermyn.

Oh, my dear Diana—I've been running after you everywhere. How very inconsiderate! [*Kissing her.*] How are you, my darling?

Mrs. Jermyn.

I'm not very well, Spencer, thank you.

Spencer Jermyn.

You look white. [*Seeing* Allan.] Hullo, you've found my boy, then?

Mrs. Jermyn.

Y-yes—we've been talking.

Spencer Jermyn.

My dear, you're surely not concerned at his size —it doesn't make *you* any older, Diana.

Mrs. Jermyn.

No, it isn't that, Spencer.

SPENCER JERMYN.

Have you been upsetting your mother, sir, before you've been in the house ten minutes?

ALLAN.

No, father.

SPENCER JERMYN.

Don't answer me, sir—don't answer me! Go away! [ALLAN *joins* MISS MOXON *and* PINCHING.] He's a fine chap, isn't he?

MRS. JERMYN.

Very.

SPENCER JERMYN.

Of course you can't judge of his excellent qualities from seeing him once, can you?

MRS. JERMYN.

Oh, no.

SPENCER JERMYN.

Wait till you've known him a week, Diana—wait till you've known him a week.

MRS. JERMYN.

Oh!

SPENCER JERMYN.

What *is* the matter, my dear girl?

MISS MOXON.

[*Coming to* MRS. JERMYN's *aid.*] How do you do, Mr. Jermyn?

SPENCER JERMYN.

Ah, Miss Moxon! Glad to get back to us, eh? Extraordinary coincidence, your living in the same house with my boy and never suspecting it. You're quite old friends, you and—what did he call himself?

               MISS MOXON.

Tom Jones.

               SPENCER JERMYN.

No, no—he didn't, he didn't!

               MISS MOXON.

John Clark.

               SPENCER JERMYN.

Tom Clark. [*To himself.*] I've turned against that woman! [PINCHING *joins* JERMYN *and* MISS MOXON.] Little did we suspect, Pinching, the other night, how near we were to the lady we both—you especially, of course—know so well.

               MISS MOXON.

Yes, but—ha, ha!—how jolly to be together here again!

               SPENCER JERMYN.

Ha! ha! ha! [*To himself.*] Wants to change the subject. That woman is deceiving poor Pinching. The singular part of it is, Miss Moxon, that when I stumbled into Mr. Brice's room in the dark I *saw* the figure of a lady.

               MISS MOXON.

[*Looking at* MRS. JERMYN.] Ah!

               SPENCER JERMYN.

[*To himself.*] I thought so. [*To* MISS MOXON.] That must have been yourself, of course.

MRS. JERMYN.

[*Approaching.*] Oh, Spencer!

SPENCER JERMYN.

One moment. [*To himself.*] I'll apply the test. [*To* MISS MOXON.] While I think of it I've a plan for this afternoon. Diana, we will drive Pinching and Miss Moxon over to Shodly to drink tea with the Warden of the Home, Mr. Brice.

[MRS. JERMYN *sinks upon the settee and* MISS MOXON *sits aghast on the ottoman.*]

SPENCER JERMYN.

[*Looking only at* MISS MOXON, *to himself.*] I'm right. Coquette! She sha'n't deceive poor Pinching any longer. I'll consult Diana. [MISS MOXON, PINCHING, *and* ALLAN *talk together.* JERMYN *sits beside* MRS. JERMYN.] Diana.

MRS. JERMYN.

Spencer.

SPENCER JERMYN.

There's something I think I ought to tell you, my dear!

MRS. JERMYN.

There's something I want to tell you, Spencer.

SPENCER JERMYN.

One moment, please, Diana. I didn't mention just now that when I entered Mr. Brice's room accidentally the other night I was unfortunate enough to witness a love episode of a very pronounced kind.

MRS. JERMYN.

Oh!

SPENCER JERMYN.

I knew you'd be shocked. The fact is that this
Mr. Brice, who is a poor, earnest kind of man, seems
to have been proposing marriage to Miss Moxon.

MRS. JERMYN.

Yes, but, Spencer, she was not—she was not—en-
couraging him!

SPENCER JERMYN.

Well, dear, it was in the dark, of course—but I
certainly didn't see any active protest on Miss Moxon's part.

MRS. JERMYN.

No, no, Spencer, you are wrong. I'll tell you all
—everything, from beginning to end. The poor
woman had no idea that Mr. Brice thought about
her seriously. Listen! Spencer—Nettles!

SPENCER JERMYN.

My darling, you know only your friend's version
of the affair. But men are loyal as well as women.
Permit me, therefore, to consider the feelings of *my*
friend—poor Pinching.

[HEWETT *enters, gives* JERMYN *a note, and they speak
together at the window.* MRS. JERMYN *beckons*
ALLAN *to her.*]

MRS. JERMYN.

Allan—my boy—you will help me, won't you?
Only help me!

ALLAN.

Of course I will—you were jolly kind to me at
Noel's.

MRS. JERMYN.

Ah, that only shows that kindness is never thrown away. Allan, steal away quietly, go into the stable, put a saddle on my Betsy—she hasn't been out since I left home and will be frightfully fresh—and *gallop* over to Shodly Heath! Tell Mr. Brice everything, Allan, and warn him, warn him that we're all coming over to tea this afternoon!

ALLAN.

All right, mother—trust to me!
[*He runs out quietly through the conservatory.*]

SPENCER JERMYN.

[*Joining* MRS. JERMYN *with a dirty scrap of paper in his hand.*] My dear, things are not going quite smoothly at Shodly Home, I'm afraid. Some of the poor fellows have walked over—a deputation they call themselves—to make some formal complaint about the behaviour of—the Warden.

MRS. JERMYN.

That's Mr. Brice!

SPENCER JERMYN.

Yes. I hope you haven't made any muddle in the affair, my dear Pinching.

PINCHING.

I!

SPENCER JERMYN.

[*To* HEWETT.] I'll see these poor men here, Hewett, at once. [HEWETT *goes out.*]

MRS. JERMYN.

[*To* MISS MOXON.]   Oh, Constance, what has happened?

MISS MOXON.

Hush, dear, hush!

SPENCER JERMYN.

[*Reading the scrap of paper.*]   Dear, oh, dear—this is most unfortunate.   Pinching, I fear—I very much fear—that your precipitate engagement of this Mr. Brice is not going to result in complete success.

PINCHING.

My dear Jermyn!

> [HEWETT *appears outside the window with* SHATTOCK, PEWS, MOULTER, *a huge bullet-headed, ruffianly-looking person, and* LYMAN, *a wizen young man with a green shade over one eye.*]

SPENCER JERMYN.

Come in, men—come in.   Diana, dear, you will be interested, I think.   Come in.

> [*The men enter and* HEWETT *retires.*]

SHATTOCK.

Ladies all!

SPENCER JERMYN.

Good - morning — good - morning.   I'm sorry to read here that you're not comfortable and happy, you men.   What do you want?

SHATTOCK.

[*With an important cough.*]   I introdooce this Depitation.

SPENCER JERMYN.

Very well—do so.

SHATTOCK.

Fust, there's me. Mr. Pews, you know and respect. Mr. Moulter never rode, but kep' the Blue Bull at Doncaster—so is one of us. He lost his license unfairly through late hours, though it was keepin' up his sister's birthday on each occasion. That he'll swear to. Mr. Lyman — step out 'ere, Bob. The name of Bob Lyman is a 'ouse'old word wherever Sport is honoured. He'll ride ag'in, Bob will, when honest men is Stooards of the Jockey Club. That's the Depitation.

SPENCER JERMYN.

Well, well, well—what is wrong with you?

SHATTOCK.

What's wrong with *us?* What is wrong with the Reverend N. Brice?

MRS. JERMYN.

[*To herself.*] Oh!

SPENCER JERMYN.

Nothing, I hope.

SHATTOCK.

Nothing! I should like his running inquired into, that's all.

SPENCER JERMYN.

Will you explain yourself? You others, speak up. [*To* LYMAN.] That little man there.

LYMAN.

Well, ladies and gentlemen, what Mr. Shattock in-

fers is the followin'. We thought we was a' enter-
ing ourselves for the Free and Easy Stakes, and we
find ourselves runnin' 'eavy in the Church o' England
Welter.

PEWS and MOULTER.

Hear, hear !

SHATTOCK.

Well put, Bob. Hear me, dear ladies. The reverend gentleman arrived yesterday afternoon, 'avin'
apperently sustained no damage on 'is journey down.
He comes up the path at Shodly 'Ome with a neat
little filly makin' all the runnin' for 'im.

SPENCER JERMYN.

Hush, hush—his niece, please.

SHATTOCK.

I 'appened to be in the porch at the time a'
throwin' up a 'armless coin or two with Mr. Pews.
" Stop that ! " he says. " Stop what ? " I says.
" Gambling ! " he says.

SPENCER JERMYN.

Good gracious ! Very arbitrary, eh, Pinching ?

SHATTOCK.

I pockets the bitter insult and I marches straight
into the drawin'-room, where a few of our gentlemen
was a' playin' parlour bowls, and I says, " Mark the
game where it stands, my lords; here's the Arch-
bishop o' Canterbury dropped in."

SPENCER JERMYN.

You shouldn't have said that.

SHATTOCK.

So the Reverend N. opinionated, for forthwith he
sticks 'isself up ag'in' the mantelpiece, and he
preaches at us from half-past three till tea-time.
Whereupon the young lady sings us a solemn air.
Well, we honcored that—not so much for the toon,
but to rile the Reverend N. And then one of our
gentlemen—'Enery 'Awkins—got melted and told
his 'istory. That did us, because 'Enery's career
'asn't been so honourable as wot ours 'as. And then
the Reverend N. lets us 'ave it agin. "Races!" he
says, "the only prize worth runnin' for is the Clear
Conscience Cup, distance, three-score years and ten.
Sport!" he says; "dooty to your neighbour, there's
sport for yer!" And then 'im and the young lady
shakes 'ands with us all round like 'ypocrites, and
retires to be weighed in, 'avin' preached ag'in' us for
three hours twenty by Benson's chronometer, bein'
the longest sermon on record.

[SHATTOCK *rejoins his companions, who receive
him approvingly.*]

MOULTER, PEWS, and LYMAN.

Well rode, Samuel, well rode!

SPENCER JERMYN.

I must say—I must say that this is *not* the treat-
ment to which any follower of the Turf should be
subjected! Pinching, I am most indignant!

SHATTOCK.

[*Looking out of window.*] Hullo, look 'ere!
'Ere's a cowardly act!

SPENCER JERMYN.

What's that?

SHATTOCK.

'E can't trust us to tell our own tale — he follows us from Shodly !

[*There is a murmur of indignation from the men. Catching sight of* NOEL, MRS. JERMYN *and* MISS MOXON *make their escape.*]

SPENCER JERMYN.

Who follows you from Shodly?

SHATTOCK.

'Im !   The Reverend N. !   'Ere he is !

[NOEL BRICE *enters with* BERTHA.]

NOEL BRICE.

Good-morning, Mr. Jermyn.

SPENCER JERMYN.

H'm !   Good-morning.

NOEL BRICE.

Bertha, dear, go and look at the flowers in the garden till I have finished.   [BERTHA *goes out through the window.*]   These men, Mr. Jermyn, knowing my intention to report the conduct of some of their number, are evidently here to defend themselves in advance.   I am glad it is so.

SPENCER JERMYN.

I beg your pardon.   These men are here, Mr. Brice, to prefer a complaint against—against—the Warden, I regret to say.

NOEL BRICE.

Indeed !

SPENCER JERMYN.

Yes, Mr. Brice, and may I ask, sir, whether——
[PINCHING *is about to steal out.*] Pinching, please,
kindly treat this affair with your usual professional
strictness.

PINCHING.

Certainly, Jermyn.

SPENCER JERMYN.

May I ask, Mr. Brice, whether you have thought
it generous to reproach these unfortunate men with
their calling, sir?

SHATTOCK.

'E 'ave !

NOEL BRICE.

I certainly have made no effort to teach them to
respect their calling. I don't like their calling, sir.

SPENCER JERMYN.

What, Mr. Brice !

SHATTOCK.

Oh, 'ark—and before Bob Lyman too !

SPENCER JERMYN.

Pinching, take notes of this, please.

PINCHING.

[*Hastily.*] I was just thinking of doing something
of that sort, Jermyn.

K

SPENCER JERMYN.

But, good gracious, Mr. Brice ! Do you forget the wording of my manifesto in *The Seraphim* ?

NOEL BRICE.

No, I recollect it perfectly.

SPENCER JERMYN.

[*Losing his patience.*] Very well then, sir, is your behaviour to these unfortunate persons consistent with a thorough sympathy with our National Sports and Pastimes ?

NOEL BRICE.

No—indeed it is not.

SPENCER JERMYN.

You admit it ! Bless my soul and body, sir ! Then do you mean to stand there and tell me to my face that you don't detect an elevating tendency in Horse-racing ?

NOEL BRICE.

I regret, sir, that my observations have not informed me of such a tendency.

SPENCER JERMYN.

Where is your letter—where is your letter ?
[*In his endeavours to find the letter he drops his cigar-case upon the floor.*]

SPENCER JERMYN.

Devil take the things ! [*To* NOEL.] I beg your pardon. Where's the letter ? Here it is. Your letter, sir,

NOEL BRICE.

My letter, sir.

SPENCER JERMYN.

[*Referring to the letter.*] May I ask you, Mr. Brice, if this attitude is consistent with a delight— a *delight, sir*—in accepting the Wardenship of my much-needed Home ?

NOEL BRICE.

No, sir, it is not—for I cannot conscientiously affirm that the Home at Shodly is a much-needed institution.

SPENCER JERMYN.

[*Beside himself, holding out the letter.*] Is that your letter ?

NOEL BRICE.

Certainly—that is my letter.

SPENCER JERMYN.

Then I'm d—— [*To* NOEL.] I beg your pardon. Pinching ! Pinching—you are my solicitor. I knew your father too. It will be both a professional and a friendly act if you will endeavour to prevent my losing entire control over myself. Pinching, what can I say to this man ? Good lord, Pinching, what shall I do ?

PINCHING.

H'm ! Ask Mr. Brice to read, word for word, his own letter. [*To himself.*] Now I *have* done something !

SPENCER JERMYN.

[*Handing the letter to* NOEL.] Your clear head is invaluable, Pinching.

NOEL BRICE.

[*Reading the letter.*] "My Dear Sir." My Dear Sir!   [*He reads the letter to himself.*]

SPENCER JERMYN.

There, sir! there! there!

NOEL BRICE.

Why, what—— Oh! What is the meaning of this?

SPENCER JERMYN.

I should be glad to know, Mr. Brice.

NOEL BRICE.

This is no letter of mine! Surely you don't—— Stop, sir—yes, this is my signature—I have signed this—it *is* my letter.

SPENCER JERMYN.

Now, Mr. Brice, you will perhaps offer some explanation.

NOEL BRICE.

I cannot. How—how can I explain—this?

SPENCER JERMYN.

That letter is evidently written at your dictation.

NOEL BRICE.

Yes. But the matter of it is not inspired by any thought or word of mine.

SPENCER JERMYN.

Do you mean, sir, that you have been made a fool of—that *I* have been made a fool of?

NOEL BRICE.

Mr. Jermyn, I have accepted a post for which my opinions and sympathies quite unfit me. If you think I owe you an apology, I offer it freely. I make an appeal to you. I ask you to allow me to destroy this letter, and to turn my back upon Shodly Heath without delay. Mr. Jermyn, let me destroy this letter!

SPENCER JERMYN.

Excuse me, sir—not just yet. My letter, please. [NOEL *returns the letter.*] Whatever injury has been done you, Mr. Brice, is more than doubled by the affront which the perpetrator of this joke has put upon me. I demand to know the name of the actual writer of this letter.

NOEL BRICE.

I regret that I cannot give it—I cannot give it.

SPENCER JERMYN.

You refuse to give it?

NOEL BRICE.

I refuse.

SPENCER JERMYN.

Take your men away for a moment, Mr. Shattock. Wait outside, please.

SHATTOCK.

Examine his pedigree, dear gentlemen !

SPENCER JERMYN.

Go away !

SHATTOCK.

Look at his mouth, dear gentlemen !

SPENCER JERMYN.

Go away!

SHATTOCK.

The Depitation then withdroo.

[SHATTOCK, PEWS, MOULTER, *and* LYMAN *go out.*]

SPENCER JERMYN.

Mr. Brice, will you be good enough to inform me if this letter is the handiwork of a lady ?

NOEL BRICE.

When I tell you that it *was* written by a lady whom I—respect, don't you see that it should be destroyed—destroyed ! [*To* PINCHING.] Sir, if you have any influence over Mr. Jermyn, will you add your earnest request to mine that this letter should be torn to shreds and forgotten ?

PINCHING.

· Certainly. I do urge Mr. Jermyn most strongly to destroy the letter and let the matter drop.

SPENCER JERMYN.

Pinching, you are. probably less my solicitor than my friend. It is in the latter capacity that I fear I am going to give you considerable pain.

PINCHING.

Jermyn !

SPENCER JERMYN.

Now, Mr. Brice, will you forgive my asking you if the lady who wrote that letter is engaged to be married to you ?

NOEL BRICE.

Sir !

SPENCER JERMYN.

You'd rather not answer ?

NOEL BRICE.

I will answer you—the lady is *not* engaged to be married to me.

SPENCER JERMYN.

[*Grasping* PINCHING's *hand.*] I am delighted to hear it ! My dear Pinching ! [*Turning to* NOEL.] My good sir ! She has refused you ?

NOEL BRICE.

No, sir, she has *not* refused me.

SPENCER JERMYN.

Not refused you. Poor Pinching ! Sir, I am sorry to deduce from your statement that you are awaiting this lady's decision ?

NOEL BRICE.

I will tell you no more, Mr. Jermyn. Will you destroy that letter ?

SPENCER JERMYN.

Stop, Mr. Brice, please. Pinching, my dear boy, in resenting the gross insult which has been put upon me I find I must deal a severe blow, not to you alone, but to that gentleman also. Pinching, oblige me by asking Miss Moxon to join us.

NOEL BRICE.

Miss Moxon! Did you say—Miss Moxon?

SPENCER JERMYN.

Pinching.

PINCHING.

Pardon me, Jermyn—as your *friend* I would rather do nothing of the kind.

NOEL BRICE.

Miss Moxon here—in your house!

SPENCER JERMYN.

Certainly. Shall I ring for Miss Moxon, Pinching, or would you prefer my seeking her?

PINCHING.

No, no—wait one moment.
[*He goes quickly into the conservatory.*]

NOEL BRICE.

What is Miss Moxon doing here? What is she doing here?

SPENCER JERMYN.

Miss Moxon is a friend of my wife's, and she has just returned to my house from yours.

NOEL BRICE.

But this gentleman, Mr. Pinching—she is nothing to him?

SPENCER JERMYN.

I regret to tell you, Mr. Brice, that Mr. Pinching and Miss Moxon are affianced lovers.

NOEL BRICE.

Ah!

[MISS MOXON *enters quickly, followed by* PINCHING.]

SPENCER JERMYN.

[*With the letter in his hand.*] Madam, you will allow me to express my deep sorrow at the position I feel justified in adopting toward a friend of Mrs. Jermyn's. With your relations with these two gentlemen I have perhaps little to do——

NOEL BRICE.

Stop, sir!

SPENCER JERMYN.

Hush, please! But with the writer of this letter I have a distinct reckoning to make. Madam, your sense of humour may be more acute and your notions of jesting more practical than my own. But, however greatly you may be my superior in these respects, I call into question your taste in placing that gentleman in the position he now occupies, and in ridiculing a scheme of charity which ignorance must have robbed you of the privilege of understanding. [*Handing* NOEL *the letter.*] Mr. Brice, I have done with that letter.

NOEL BRICE.

Pardon me, Mr. Jermyn, but may I ask this lady's name?

SPENCER JERMYN.

That lady's name !

NOEL BRICE.

Because if it is not that gentleman's duty to defend her from the charges you have brought against her it is *mine.*

PINCHING.

It *is* my duty ! I was just thinking of saying so !

SPENCER JERMYN.

Do you mean to stand there and tell me that you don't recognize the lady who has resided in your house for nearly a fortnight? .

PINCHING.

Jermyn, she has done nothing of the kind !

SPENCER JERMYN.

You'll drive me mad amongst you ! [*To* NOEL.] You don't deny that that lady was recently your niece's companion ?

NOEL BRICE.

Certainly, I deny it.

SPENCER JERMYN.

Madam, have you not just returned from Mr. Brice's lodgings ?

MISS MOXON.

Oh, no, Mr. Jermyn—I have never seen Mr. Brice till this moment.

SPENCER JERMYN.

Never seen him! Never seen him! Why, the night before last I saw you see him!

PINCHING.

Jermyn, believe me, you don't know anything about it!

SPENCER JERMYN.

Not know anything about it! (*To* NOEL.) Was Miss Constance Moxon ever your niece's companion?

NOEL BRICE.

She was, sir.

SPENCER JERMYN.

Then how dare you all——

NOEL BRICE.

She was—but, Mr. Jermyn, you know that that lady is *not* Miss Constance Moxon.

SPENCER JERMYN.

Not Miss Constance Moxon! Good heavens!

PINCHING.

Yes, she is!

MISS MOXON.

Yes, I am!

[BERTHA *appears at the window.*]

BERTHA.

Uncle! Uncle Noel! I've found her! I've found her!

NOEL BRICE.

Found her!

BERTHA.

Miss Moxon! She's here! She's here! Miss Moxon!

NOEL BRICE.

[*Turning to the others.*] I told you so! What trick are you all playing me?

SPENCER JERMYN.

Miss Moxon!

[BERTHA *enters, dragging* MRS. JERMYN *by the hand.*]

BERTHA.

Uncle Noel, look here!

NOEL BRICE.

Miss Moxon!

SPENCER JERMYN.

Miss Moxon! That is Mrs. Jermyn—that is my wife, sir!

NOEL BRICE.

Your *wife!* Miss Moxon, your wife!

SPENCER JERMYN.

Why, you don't mean that this is the lady who—— Oh!

[HEWETT *enters, supporting* ALLAN, *who is limping.*]

HEWETT.

All right, sir—young gentleman got thrown!

ALLAN.

[*Sinking on to the settee.*] Noel—mother!

PINCHING.

[*Quietly to* Miss Moxon.] I kept it from him as long as I possibly could—nobody could have done more.

BERTHA.

Oh, uncle, Allan is hurt! Allan!

HEWETT.

He's all right, miss. Young gentleman got Betsy out of the stable on his own account. He come off beautifully, just by Pinnock's Gate—never saw a gentleman come off neater. [HEWETT *retires.*]

SPENCER JERMYN.

Mr. Brice, do I understand you to tell me that Mrs. Jermyn is the lady you have hitherto supposed to be Miss Moxon?

NOEL BRICE.

Mrs. Jermyn *is* the lady I have known as Miss Moxon.
[*He turns away and leans against the mantlepiece with his head bowed.*]

SPENCER JERMYN.

Diana.

MRS. JERMYN.

Spencer.

SPENCER JERMYN.

Then you, and not Miss Moxon, have been acting as companion to this young lady during my absence from Odlum House?

MRS. JERMYN.

Yes, Spencer!

SPENCER JERMYN.

And I understand, Miss Moxon, that this has been with your connivance and assistance?

MISS MOXON.

Yes!

SPENCER JERMYN.

While at the same time you have remained my guest?

MISS MOXON.

Yes, Mr. Jermyn!

SPENCER JERMYN.

And you have known all this, Allan?

ALLAN.

Found it out this morning, father!

SPENCER JERMYN.

And you, Pinching?

PINCHING.

H'm! I learned the state of affairs yesterday.

SPENCER JERMYN.

[*Looking round from one to the other.*] Thank you!

ALLAN.

You know, father, you've only been home about half an hour—there hasn't been time to tell you all the news.

SPENCER JERMYN.

Be silent!

ALLAN.

[*Quietly to* BERTHA.] Bertha, my knee is awfully bad—come and walk about in the garden.
[*They steal out through the window.*]

PINCHING.

If my action has been at all undecided in this business, Jermyn——

SPENCER JERMYN.

Mr. Pinching !

PINCHING.

I hope you will attribute it to my good fortune in being engaged to one of the ladies concerned.

MISS MOXON.

I am afraid *I* don't come out of it as well as I should like to, Mr. Jermyn.

SPENCER JERMYN.

Excellently, Miss Moxon. I thought you had been guilty of a joke—I find it is nothing of the kind.

MISS MOXON.

Oh, take me away ! I'm not used to unkindness and can't bear it ! Take me away !
[PINCHING *leads her out through the conservatory.*]

SPENCER JERMYN.

Mr. Brice. A few moments ago you asked me to destroy the letter which you now hold in your hand,

and I refused to do so. I am now ashamed to discover that it is a letter written by my wife to which your signature has been obtained by unfair means. Is that so, Diana?

MRS. JERMYN.

It is so, Spencer.

SPENCER JERMYN.

I am in your hands, Mr. Brice—what do you intend to do with that letter?

NOEL BRICE.

Return it to you, Mr. Jermyn, thinking you may some day see in it nothing but the evidence of an impulsive lady's compassion and tender-heartedness towards a very poor man.

[*He hands* JERMYN *the letter and walks away to the veranda.*]

MRS. JERMYN.

Spencer.

SPENCER JERMYN.

Diana.

MRS. JERMYN.

That is the truth. I wanted to aid Mr. Brice, who is so badly off. I wrote the letter hoping to obtain his signature fairly, but when he had signed it in ignorance it fell into Mr. Pinching's hands. Oh, you see what a plight philanthropy has brought me to!

SPENCER JERMYN.

Unfortunately everybody can see it.

Mrs. Jermyn.

I know I'm a spectacle. It was worse than indiscreet of me to take Constance's place at Mr. Brice's.

Spencer Jermyn.

I won't contradict you.

Mrs. Jermyn.

Thank you. I did it on the despairing discovery that you couldn't, wouldn't sympathize with my aims.

Spencer Jermyn.

Oh!

Mrs. Jermyn.

Yes. But even then I didn't let anybody but you take me to London.

Spencer Jermyn.

Don't jest, madam.

Mrs. Jermyn.

I won't, dear. Perhaps because I was in Mrs. Landon's bonnet and waterproof you did not recognize me.

Spencer Jermyn.

Diana!

Mrs. Jermyn.

Yes, Nettles, and you paid for my ticket to town —but only third class. And then, you must remember, when I *did* get to Mr. Brice's there was the boy—our son—to watch over his mother. And what has been my greatest fault? Why, procuring

L

a Warden for the much-needed Home! Oh, don't
look like that, Nettles! The Home at Shodly Heath
is a flourishing establishment—in your hour of
triumph pity my complete collapse! I thought
that a ragged, uncombed, unwashed community was
my sphere. Spencer, I have found out it isn't!
[*Crying on his shoulder.*] Surely you can feel for a
philanthropist less fortunate than yourself! [NOEL
comes into the room.] If I've done no good I've done
no harm—— [*She sees* NOEL.] Except—— Oh,
Spencer, you know the mistake that has occurred.
Say what you like to me—but beg *his* pardon, for I
- can't.

SPENCER JERMYN.

Mr. Brice, Mrs. Jermyn tells me I am to beg your
pardon. I do so. I have married a very foolish
headstrong lady—I beg your pardon. Mrs. Jermyn
keeps your niece company and assists you in your
parish work without my permission—I beg your
pardon. In the meantime you fall in love with my
wife, sir, and you ultimately propose marriage to
her in my presence—I beg your pardon.

MRS. JERMYN.

Oh, dear! Oh, dear! You're not doing it properly!

NOEL BRICE.

Mr. Jermyn, the tone you speak in spares me the
pain of thinking that you believe an apology is neces-
sary. As for my—mistake, it is slighter than you
imagine.

SPENCER JERMYN.

Slighter?

NOEL BRICE.

Yes, sir. The only great mistake possible in proposing marriage is to select an unworthy object. I fell into no such error. I believed Miss Moxon to be a generous, warm-hearted lady, whom any man should be proud to call his wife. I thought that, and I think it still!

SPENCER JERMYN.

[*Pointing to* Mrs. JERMYN.] But your Miss Moxon is Mrs. Jermyn, Mr. Brice!

NOEL BRICE.

So I find—and upon that I congratulate you with all my heart.

SPENCER JERMYN.

Eh? Oh—thank you!

NOEL BRICE.

Before I leave your house, Mr. Jermyn, I wish to discharge the duty which brought me here. [*Going to the window and calling.*] Shattock!

[SHATTOCK *appears at the window with* PEWS, MOULTER, *and* LYMAN. SHATTOCK *advances into the room.*]

SHATTOCK.

Don't listen to 'im, lady and gentleman—he's a outsider, lady and gentleman!

NOEL BRICE.

I desire to tell you, Mr. Jermyn, that you are harbouring at your house at Shodly a set of unprincipled ruffians, to whom the man who befriends them is an object of contempt and ridicule.

SHATTOCK.

It was 'Opkinson wot said you had a tile off, sir!

SPENCER JERMYN.

A tile off! Send Hopkinson away!

NOEL BRICE.

[*Taking a written paper from his pocket and giving it to* JERMYN.] I am going to hand over to Mr. Jermyn a letter written by you, Shattock, which was intercepted by the man Hawkins and given to me last night.

SHATTOCK.

A letter! Wot letter? [*To* JERMYN. Don't 'eed it, sir—don't 'eed it! It's a forgery, sir—there's a low lot in the 'Ome!

SPENCER JERMYN.

[JERMYN *takes the paper from* NOEL *and reads it.*] Diana! This is a letter from this man Shattock to a person named Emanuel, of Newmarket, offering to dispose surreptitiously of eight brass candlesticks and all the cutlery and linen in the Shodly Home.

MRS. JERMYN.

Oh, Spencer!

SHATTOCK.

I'm learnin' to write, sir—it's my exercise, sir!

SPENCER JERMYN.

Let every man-jack of you be out of Shodly Farm by four o'clock to-day, or I'll put this letter in the hands of the police !

[PEWS, LYMAN, *and* MOULTER *sneak away.*]

SHATTOCK.

[*With scorn.*] The police — *you* wouldn't get smiled at, would you ?

NOEL BRICE.

Come, my man, I'll walk with you to the lodge gate.

SHATTOCK.

What, Mr. Spencer Jermyn, did you think you was a goin' to patronize men o' the position of Bob Lyman and me ! Let this be a solemn lesson to you. Why you ought to be warned off every respectable race-course—you foolish, vain old gentleman !

NOEL BRICE.

Now, Mr. Shattock, please ?

SHATTOCK.

'Ere ! Am I to be paid for my time or not ?

SPENCER JERMYN.

If you don't leave this room I'll ring for my servants.

SHATTOCK.

Hah ! There's orstentation !

[SHATTOCK *goes out through the window and disappears, followed by* NOEL.]

SPENCER JERMYN.

The wretches! The ungrateful wretches! The sleepless hours this scheme has cost me! Nothing so complete had ever been organized. And then to think—only to think—that it shouldn't work after all.

MRS. JERMYN.

Oh, Spencer! Your philanthropy, like mine, is an awful failure—let our common misfortunes bring us together. Nettles!

SPENCER JERMYN.

But look at my position! A little while ago I had a Home without a Warden, now I've a Warden without a Home!

MRS. JERMYN.

Write to Canon Carver and beg him to do something for Mr. Brice.

SPENCER JERMYN.

I will—something a long way off.
[ALLAN *and* BERTHA *appear at the window.*]

ALLAN.

Father! those Shodly Heath men are picking all our flowers.

SPENCER JERMYN.

Let them pluck them up by the roots.

MRS. JERMYN.
[*Pointing to* ALLAN *and* BERTHA.] Spencer—look. I suppose you guess what that means?

SPENCER JERMYN.

The scamp—yes.

MRS. JERMYN.

Well, then, why shouldn't we — both of us — re-
build the old farm-house at Shodly and furnish it
sumptuously as a home——

SPENCER JERMYN.

Another Home !

MRS. JERMYN.

A home for Allan and Bertha.

SPENCER JERMYN.

Allan's home at Shodly, eh? That's *something*
like my scheme !

MRS. JERMYN.

It *is* your scheme. And then, in time, when there
are three or four babbling babies rolling upon the
grass——

SPENCER JERMYN.

Yes, but that's *your* scheme, Diana.

MRS. JERMYN.

It's *something* like my scheme. Don't you see,
Nettles—we shall please each other at last? [PINCH-
ING *and* MISS MOXON *appear outside the window.*]
Spencer, are you still thinking that you can't for-
give me?

SPENCER JERMYN.

No, Diana—I am thinking that in the future I

shall be seldom seen at Epsom and Ascot and Goodwood and Doncaster.

MRS. JERMYN.

Hush, Spencer—why?

SPENCER JERMYN.

Ah, because I mustn't leave my wife alone any
more, Diana.

MRS. JERMYN.

No, Nettles, but—— [*Taking his hand affectionately.*] you must always take her with you.

THE END.

Printed by BALLANTYNE HANSON & CO.
London and Edinburgh

A Selection

FROM

MR. WM. HEINEMANN'S LIST

February 1892.

—•◦•—

The Crown Copyright Series.

The changed conditions of publishing in the English-speaking countries, brought about by the American Copy-right Legislation of 1891, *have made it possible—without doing injustice to the authors—to issue new and original works of fiction in a form immediately accessible to the large class of readers who are unwilling to be permanently and entirely beholden to the Circulating Libraries. Mr. Heinemann has therefore made arrangements with a number of the first and most popular authors of to-day,*

ENGLISH, AMERICAN, AND COLONIAL,

which will enable him to issue new and original works of theirs in a Series to be known as the CROWN COPY-RIGHT SERIES at a uniform price of FIVE SHILLINGS per volume.

These novels will not pass through an expensive two or three volume edition, but they will be obtainable at the Circulating Libraries as well as at all Booksellers and Bookstalls.

The following volumes are now ready:—

ACCORDING TO ST. JOHN. By AMÉLIE RIVES, Author of "The Quick or the Dead," &c.

THE PENANCE OF PORTIA JAMES. By "TASMA," Author of "Uncle Piper of Piper's Hill,"&c.

INCONSEQUENT LIVES. A Village Chroni-cle, Shewing how certain Folk set out for El Dorado, What they Attempted, and What they Attained. By J. H. PEARCE, Author of "Esther Pentreath," &c.

A QUESTION OF TASTE. By MAARTEN MAARTENS, Author of "The Sin of Joost Avelingh," &c.
[*In the Press.*]

Heinemann's 3s. 6d. Novels.

UNCLE PIPER OF PIPER'S HILL. By
"TASMA," Author of "The Penance of Portia James," &c.

A MARKED MAN. Some Episodes in his Life.
By ADA CAMBRIDGE.
Pall Mall.—"Contains one of the best written stories of a *mésalliance* that is to be found in modern fiction."

IN THE VALLEY. By HAROLD FREDERIC.
Illustrated.
Athenæum.—"A novel deserving to be read."

THE THREE MISS KINGS. By ADA
CAMBRIDGE.
British Weekly.—"A novel to be bought and kept for re-reading on languid summer afternoons or stormy winter evenings.

PRETTY MISS SMITH. By FLORENCE
WARDEN.
Punch.—"Since the 'House on the Marsh,' I have not read a more exciting tale."

A ROMANCE OF THE CAPE FRONTIER.
By BERTRAM MITFORD.
Observer.—" A rattling tale—genial, healthy, and spirited."

THE BONDMAN. By HALL CAINE.
Academy.—"A splendid novel."

A MODERN MARRIAGE. By the MARQUISE
CLARA LANZA.
Queen.—" A powerful story."

LOS CERRITOS. A Romance of the Modern
Time. By GERTRUDE FRANKLIN ATHERTON.
Athenæum.—"A decidedly charming romance."

DAUGHTERS OF MEN. By HANNAH LYNCH.
Author of " The Prince of the Glades," &c.   [*Shortly.*

New Works of Fiction.

NOT ALL IN VAIN. By ADA CAMBRIDGE,
Author of " A Marked Man," &c.

THE SCAPEGOAT. By HALL CAINE, Author
of " The Bondman." Fourth Edition. In Two Vols.

MAMMON. By Mrs. ALEXANDER, Author of
" The Wooing O't," &c. In Three Vols.

MEA CULPA. A Woman's Last Word. By
HENRY HARLAND (Sidney Luska). Author of " As it was
Written." In Three Volumes, crown 8vo.

COME FORTH ! A Story of the Time of Christ.
By ELIZABETH STUART PHELPS and HERBERT D. WARD,
In One Volume, imperial 16mo, 7s. 6d.

THE MASTER OF THE MAGICIANS. A
Novel. By ELIZABETH STUART PHELPS and HERBERT
D. WARD. In One Volume, imperial 16mo, 7s. 6d.

THE MOMENT AFTER. A Tale of the
Unseen. By ROBERT BUCHANAN. Popular Edition,
crown 8vo, 1s.

In Preparation.

WOMAN AND THE MAN. By ROBERT
BUCHANAN. In Two Vols.

LITTLE JOHANNES. A Fairy Tale. By
F. VAN EEDEN. Translated from the Dutch, by CLARA
BELL, with an Introduction by ANDREW LANG, and Illus-
trations. In One Volume.

THE TOWER OF TADDEO. By OUIDA,
Author of "Two Little Wooden Shoes," &c.

ORIOLE'S DAUGHTER. By JESSIE FOTHER-
GILL, Author of " The First Violin," &c. In Three Vols.

**COME LIVE WITH ME AND BE MY
LOVE.** By ROBERT BUCHANAN.

THE WHITE FEATHER. By "TASMA." In
Three Vols.

A BATTLE AND A BOY. By BLANCHE
WILLIS HOWARD, Author of "Guenn," &c.

Miscellaneous.

THE WORD OF THE LORD UPON THE.

WATERS. Sermons read by the Emperor of Germany while on his Voyages to the Land of the Midnight Sun. Composed by Dr. RICHTER. Small 4to, cloth, 2s. 6d.

THE LITTLE MANX NATION. By HALL

CAINE, Author of "The Bondman." Crown 8vo, cloth, 3s. 6d.; paper, 2s. 6d.

GIRLS AND WOMEN. By E. CHESTER.

Pott 8vo, 2s. 6d., or gilt extra, 3s. 6d.

GOSSIP IN A LIBRARY. By EDMUND GOSSE.

Second Edition. Crown 8vo, bevelled boards, 7s. 6d.

CONTENTS : Camden's Britannia. A Mirror for Magistrates. A Poet in Prison. Death's Duel. Gerard's Herbal. Phara-mond. A Volume of Old Plays. A Censor of Poets. Lady Winchilsea's Poems. Amasia. Love and Business. What Ann Lang read. Cats. Smart's Poems. Pompey the Little. John Buncle. Beau Nash. The Diary of a Loverof Literature. Peter Bell and his Tormentors. The Fancy. Ultra-crepi-darius. The Duke of Rutland's Poems. Ionica. The Shaving of Shagpat.

WOMAN—THROUGH A MAN'S EYE-

GLASS. By MALCOLM C. SALAMAN. With Illus-trations by DUDLEY HARDY.   . *[In the Press.*

THE WORKS OF HEINRICH HEINE.

Translated by CHARLES G. LELAND, F.R.L.S., M.A. Volume I.—Florentine Nights, Schnabelewopski. The Rabbi of Bacharach, and Shakespeare's Maidens and Women. Volumes II. and III., Pictures of Travel. In Two Volumes. Volume IV., The Book of Songs. Volumes V. and VI., Germany. In Two Volumes. Crown 8vo, 5s. each.